Journey Back When

ORMA®
Columbus Circle
PO Box 20928
New York, New York 10023
www.wdmoore.co

ISBN: 0615746365
ISBN-13: 9780615746364
ISBN (ebook): 978-0-615-86671-0

Journey Back When

a novel by

W. D. Moore

In memory of Arthur Banks (Uncle Spooky) and Daniel H. Coleman

For Still

I would like to thank:
Crystal Blake
Anthony R.H. Gerard
Leesa E. Grant
Kelli Knight
Jeannie Maddox
Angie L. Moore
Ana A. Rodriquez
Jackson Taylor
Jeannette Topar
And always—Mickey

Prologue

At this time, she knew he would, but how could she stop him, her son. In 1969, he was running away from home at fourteen. Tired hips hopped off the green velvet sofa and strutted to the kitchen where she felt safe. Strong legs paced circles on the pink, posh rug, while John Jr. placed his bag in the hallway where she could clearly see his intentions. Proud son, determined, with ten dollars in his pockets, he could purchase a cheap seat at the Greyhound Bus station in downtown Atlanta. He wouldn't need to hitch a ride to Florida; he could sit on the bus, forget his heart. Megan, his mother, model-looking—her greatest weapon was her wondrous talent for cooking food so that no human being could walk out of her home. The smell and sound of her skillet-fried chicken slowly lay in her mother's pan, the fire popping left and right—even the neighbors' ankles were weak walking by. But John Jr. couldn't smell her cooking. He didn't eat lunch because he was studying for his final examination at Eden High School. He had no dinner, and didn't even want to take that damn exam tomorrow to attend the distinguished Morehouse College. John Jr. aspired to be like his father and travel around the world. He often told his friends, "My dad is an officer in the United States Air Force; he is on tours in Frankfurt Germany, Paris France—and for piña coladas, he jets to Florida. Some nights, John Jr. could not sleep, and when he did, he dreamed of his dad's soulful journeys, adventures, heroics of being a fighter pilot.

Megan managed to move her eyes briefly away from John Jr. as he motioned to leave the house. His one duffle bag in hand, he hurried to the bus stop. Her heart was pounding, but patient restraint ran through her body; she prayed he would return. A mother's mind was made up—he would stay in Atlanta and attend college where she could take care of him. John, her husband, has been on a long tour assignment for twelve months, and now, John Jr. wants to leave home, leave possibilities to happen, leave her hopeful heart. Megan wrapped the white lace and polka-dot apron around her waist. She saw two baby blackbirds savaging food she had left for them yesterday on the windowsill. "How happy they look," she thought. "They are home." She turned to watch her son wait for the A60 bus. Tears were dry, body rejuvenated, her staying power was strong. It was ten o'clock at night; the last bus ran at nine o'clock on Fridays.

PART I

1

The year was 1972. It was after the light of dawn—Megan was listening to the firm breeze, being far away underneath her pressed cotton sheets.

John Jr. awoke to anxiety; he overslept. Football practice was at eight o'clock in the morning. His feet stumbled on university brochures, collegiate dictionaries, math books, sports magazines. He slipped, fell, jumped. His eyes met the clock at seven-forty-five. He grabbed his pants and jacket. Racing into his parents' bedroom, he said, "Mom, you didn't wake me; I'm going to be late for practice." Megan lifted her head from the sheets.

"John Jr., it's Sunday. You don't have football practice today. Go back to bed. I'll make breakfast in a few minutes."

"Mom, we have practice this Sunday, because it's a special Sunday. Coach wants us to throw balls with a new player on the team."

"John Jr., I don't recall Coach Elmore telephoning about practice today."

"Mom, I told Dad yesterday. He said it was okay." Megan sat upright in her bed.

"Your father didn't tell me. He left early this morning. He didn't wake me up...at least, I don't remember. He didn't say anything, and since I didn't know, you can't go."

"Mom, that's not fair. I can't miss practice. Everybody will laugh at me."

"What about the Tornado watch later? How could your coach call practice today?"

"Mom it's just a little misty, the sun is already out."

Megan searched under the bed for her pink feather slippers. She snatched her white linen robe off the floor. "Go on then, I'll save your breakfast, put it in the oven for you." John Jr. tied his running shoes, kissed his mother's cold cheeks.

"Mom, I don't want breakfast, only pie."

"You will have to eat your breakfast first before you can have some pie."

John Jr. ran out the door, "Okay Mom." She looked at him for a few minutes; the next minute he was gone.

She stood in the doorway, watched her son, and reminisced about when they moved on Chester Street—where tree-lined, split-leveled houses, wide front porches with rocking chairs, and back porches with gardens looked alike. Except—they have a grand willow tree in their back-yard, and multiple green birdhouses around the outside of their yellow house. That weekend in 1954, her next door neighbor Mrs. Vinnie Rose declared, "Your yard is two-tenths wider than ours. I don't understand how that could have happened, since we sold you the property."

John and Megan were cleaning their backyard. Mrs. Rose added, "You newcomers don't know what this street used to be like. I remember when it was just land and dirt road. Mr. Rose bought this land over thirty years ago. Relatives thought we were crazy." She waved at John and said, "Mr. Smith, I need to sit down for a spell; my knees are killing me this morning." He relaxed the red wheelbarrow, walked over to her, turned over a wooden rocking chair that was covered in a forest of leaves. She sat down. "Thank you," she said. She looked over at Megan. "Come over here, Mrs. Smith. You can't hear me from way over there." Megan dusted the leaves off her shirt stood close to John. They held hands.

"My husband never wanted to sell your lot. I'm sure glad he did. Daniel kept hemming and hawing and saying he was going extend our house. He reclined all day in his Windsor armchair, played poker, lost money. Of course, there were other reasons I wanted to sell, but never mind that. Anyway, I am glad we have you for neighbors—especially you, Mrs. Smith, because we love the smell of your cooking." Megan kissed Mrs. Rose's rosy cheeks. John kissed his wife's peach and cream lips."

"Good morning, Megan," Agnes Portman yelled cheerfully while opening the door to her family's Buick Sport Wagon.

"Oh, good morning, Agnes," Megan replied warningly, "I didn't see you." She waved and closed the door; strolled up to the walnut staircase.

In her bedroom, she opened her vanity drawer, and searched for her pearl hair clip. She gazed at the white chiffon curtains; the weather was changing to summertime cool. Manicured hands caressed her face, love birds were singing, as she strolled to the window. Her eyes glanced at the birds. They moved diagonally across Mrs. Rose's window. A dark shadow watched her. She pulled down the shade. "I was not imagining it," she thought. "I know someone is there. Could it be Mrs. Rose's nephew? John mentioned Mrs. Rose had a relative living with her, but I have not seen him. Why didn't John wake me up before he flew out to another foreign country? It's Sunday, my son is at football practice, my husband is never home, and I am alone. I heard him leave around five this morning. I didn't have the energy to get out of bed; I never like saying goodbye. Why can't I have a husband who is home every day? I should have been nice. I'm sick of it, sick of everything being the same."

She unfastened her pearl clip, waves fell half length at her back. She disrobed and stepped into the shower. Fifteen minutes later, water droplets trailed her in the bedroom. Body lotion in hand, she sensed the shadow and clung to her comfy robe. "This is ridiculous. This is my house," she said. "I wish my husband was with me. I want him. He didn't tell me when he was returning. He still hasn't called me."

Like magic, the telephone rang. "Now he calls," she said. "Hello...John." It clicked. She held it for a moment. "Maybe John got disconnected; I am going to ignore my neighbor. I might mention him to John though." She combed her wet hair and moisturized her face. The telephone rang. It rang twice more. On the fourth ring she said, "Hello."

"Megan Baby," John said. "Sorry, I didn't get to call you sooner. I had a meeting with Colonel Saddleback. I'll call you when I arrive in Spain. This may be a short tour." She was quiet. John continued, "Baby don't be mad. I miss you even more when you don't love me."

"John, did you call me a few minutes ago?"

"No Baby, I'm calling now."

"John, I was tired this morning. I'll make sure you get a big hug when you come home."

"That's all, Baby," he sighed.

"John, don't start."

"Alright, Baby, I'll be home soon. Got to go! I love you."

"I love you to." Megan's body was soft, her hair wrapped in a towel. She walked to the closet, stopped, and faced the window shade. In a few seconds, she reached for her pink linen dress with thin black stain straps. "I think I'll take a peace pie over to Mrs. Rose's today." She dressed, eyes diverted to the window, dazzled, she was in the mirror. "I remember when I was a young girl of six, and people kept telling me how pretty I was," she said. "I didn't know what pretty meant. I asked my momma, Lina.

She was ironing Daddy Windom's shirts, and I said, 'Momma do you think I am pretty?' 'Yes,' she replied, 'you're my Georgia peach.'"

She rolled up the window shade, enjoyed fresh air on her flawless skin, luminous face. Suddenly, their eyes met. Neither pair of eye moved. She rolled down the shade. She inhaled a deep breath, exhaled, "he can't be Mrs. Rose's

3

nephew. He looks like a man, not a boy," she thought. Still, she promenaded down the staircase.

In her kitchen, she rinsed peaches and pulled eggs and milk out of the refrigerator. Her feverish fingers rolled out the pie crust on the pastry board. She pushed aside the vase of daffodils on the wood countertop. "I'll make two peach cobbler pies today," she murmured. In twenty minutes, the pies were in the oven. She cooked pork sausages on the stove. "Let me make John Jr. his pancakes," she said. She battered the buttermilk mix in a bowl, added extra butter, two teaspoons of water. Stirring milk and blueberries rapidly, she rested for a moment, looking at her hands. The left was sticky, the right smooth.

"Eighteen years ago," she said to herself, "the same thing; the same soft hands. He kissed me, I was shocked, scared, and he did it again. I liked it. I let his tongue embrace my entire body. When our son John Jr. was born a year later, I still felt ecstasy from his soft touch.

"Days passed, nights passed, mornings started again. I remember a box of Auntie Manna's Original Pancake Mix. I was cooking breakfast. The fall leaves were beginning to turn orange; another tree's branches were as yellow as the bright sun. I was having trouble opening the box, and I used a knife to punch a hole in it. The entire box of white powder fell on my newly mopped floor. I couldn't help, but laugh out loud at myself.

"John Jr. thought I was crying; my husband thought I was crazy. We instantly started smiling, singing that song from the Supremes. Now, I don't remember the song, except, after John Jr. dashed out for school, my husband's hands grabbed me, pulled me toward him. 'I'm mad at you, he said, I wanted to stay in bed, breakfast was on your mind instead.'

"The radio played 'My Girl' by the Temptations, our special song. We danced, delighted ourselves. As the years come, time changed my heart. His special assignments: short tours or long tours—it's all the same to me.

"And yet, yesterday before dinner, he stood in the hallway looking at me bake buttermilk biscuits. I knew he was thinking how once he massaged my breast with the same kind of butter, and how we had moved on the floor. He gave me a sweet smile, drew in closer. I turned the music volume high, John became still. I was delirious, singing alone with B.B. King, 'The Thrill is Gone.' I couldn't help it—he knows how I feel, and he does nothing."

She placed John Jr.'s breakfast in the refrigerator, brewed her special southern-blend coffee. She sat at the square, block, wooden table, arms folded, clear nails caressing her skin. New memories began. "I wore this dress when his tender kisses, passionate words loved me. I miss my husband." She walked to the counter, poured her coffee, gazed at Mrs. Rose's house.

Moments afterwards, she yelled, "darn it." Black coffee stains were on her linen dress. Running to her bedroom, she stepped out of her dress, her white cotton slip, and skipped to the bathroom. Ice-cold water ran down like a water fall in the bathroom sink. "He's no longer a shadow. I saw his deep dark eyes. Are they dangerous?" she pondered.

When the telephone rang, she said, "What if it's him?" It rang again. She hesitated, "Hello."

"Mom," his hurried words said. "Coach Elmore said we have practice for another two hours."

"Okay, John Jr., that's fine," she smiled. "I'll see you for an early dinner, I guess."

The glide in her walk was regal as she roamed to her closet. She searched for another dress and found the right one. The color was purple, the fabric was rayon, and the sash pulled her small waist in tight. She stood in front of the full-length mirror. She liked what she saw—her beauty.

She entered the kitchen, poured herself another cup of coffee. She held the white "U.S. Air Force Mug" in one hand, opened the patio door, and relaxed in her wicker chair. The wind blew gently through her hair as she sipped her coffee and closed her eyes. "I don't want to think, what's the difference? He's never leaving the Air Force." She looked at her birdhouse, viewed the sparrows at play. "My true companions," she thought. Her eyes returned shut. Silently, she said, "Before John enlisted in the Air Force Reserve in 1970, he was home, we stayed in bed on Saturday mornings. John Jr. was engrossed in football practice, left by eight o'clock. John made the coffee, carried the pot to our bed. We talked about politics, pilots, and airplanes in between making love.

"In the warm afternoons, we sometimes reclined on the front porch listening to John Coltrane's The Stardust Session while enjoying cocktails—gin and tonic, John's favorite, with a juicy lime. How I miss those days. I love him; hate him until he's back again. My husband was once my best friend. He just can't get the Air Force out of his blood, and after twenty-one years, he retired, rejoined the Air Force Reserve without asking me. A week later he left.

"I would say to Miss May Perry, 'my man hunted me down, I simply gave in.' He was patient, persevered throughout my father's disapproval. Daddy Windom wanted me to attend college, become a pianist. My mother,

Lina, persuaded me to follow my heart. I loved and admired John. We were married—year later, I was pregnant with our son. It was exciting in the beginning. He was gone for weeks, then he opened that door, we would eat each other with our passion.

"One morning, weeks became months, months became a year, and I became a chambermaid. Oh, why do I continue to play back memories over and over? I rewind my mind every time, whenever he leaves for long trips. I hope he is home for Christmas that would make up for today."

Megan's wide eyes continued, "This is the best coffee I have ever made. Too bad John is not here to enjoy it with me." She caressed her hair, crossed her smooth legs. She heard the neighbors' children playing across the street, birds singing, and sweet reminders of summer in September. "Good morning, Mrs. Smith," he said.

A startled Megan immediately leaped out of her chair and glanced at her shadow a few feet away.

"I live next door with my Aunt Rose. She said she will stop by after church service to have Sunday pie with you, if that was OK with you? Oh, she also told me to tell you my name."

Megan peered intensely, pretended not to notice the power of his body. The athletic stature of his presence, she had seen on the cover of her husband's sports magazines, still, she had never been inches from a body like his. He enticed her; they inspected one another. She was surprised at her comfort with him, and embarrassed. She tied her sash tighter. "I hope you enjoy our Chester Street," she said. He blinked when a leaf fell on her chest. She brushed it off her breast.

"Yes Mrs. Smith, I like Chester Street very much. It's nice meeting you." In a short moment, he rambled, he glanced at the grass, and he stared in her eyes.

"What did you say your name was?" She laid her coffee cup down.

Blue circled back to her, put one foot on her patio steps. "My aunt calls me Blue," he said, "but my nickname is 'Big Boy Blue.'"

Megan inhaled a long breath and in a swift second said, "Tell Mrs. Rose I look forward to seeing her later, and thank you." Blue removed his foot and meandered through the orange and green leaves to his aunt's house. He stopped. His back at her, he said, "Yes, Mrs. Smith, I'll tell her."

She settled cozy in her white wicker chair, crossed her leg to the other side, and sipped her cold coffee. "What a warm and lovely day," she whispered. Her head directed to the sky, she echoed, "Blue."

2

"Playing football is the only reason to get out of bed on the weekends," John Jr. said when he threw the ball to Willie.

"Yeah, but Coach Elmore called practice at eight-thirty this morning, and the new player ain't here," Willie replied annoyingly, tossing the football to John Jr.

John Jr. caught the ball, tossed it in the air. "Coach Elmore had been hoping to win the state championship title for two decades, and every year he adds a new player who he dreams can bring him the state championship title." He hurled the ball back to Willie, and said, "Last week, Coach said, 'Son, I like the way you throw the ball. If Billy Calloway's hand is ever broken you will be next in line. It probably doesn't matter to you anyway, since you are a straight-A student, attending Morehouse next year.'"

Willie squatted on the bench and tied his shoe laces. "What do you think this new guy is like? Coach keeps talking about him. We've been here for two hours waiting for him. Didn't Coach tell him what time practice was?"

"I saw him yesterday; he lives next door to us," replied John Jr.

"Did you speak to him? I heard he's fast. Coach really believes; he's the one. What's his name anyway?"

"I don't know his name. I just saw him jumping rope in Mrs. Rose's backyard. Say, Willie, throw me the ball."

"He'll be a pro for sure," Willie returned. "Wonder why he moved to Atlanta?"

"Willie," John Jr. yelled, running fast toward the upper field, "sling it over here." The ball twirled low, John Jr. missed the catch. It landed hard on his head. His feet slipped, and he fell in a patch of muddy dirt. Willie giggled. John Jr. steamed, charged, and tackled him to the ground.

"I'm sorry John Jr., I was just fooling around," Willie chuckled. Moments became minutes, they squatted in the grass.

About fifteen minutes later, Coach Elmore yelled, "Everybody form a straight line and run around the track a quick twenty."

"I can barely move." Willie said, staring at the coach. Coach Elmore gazed at his new player running toward him. The entire team froze. Their goggled eyes were on Big Boy Blue.

"Do you see that guy?" Willie said to John Jr. "He's Hercules and how."

Coach Elmore blew his whistle and yelled, "Blue, come here, son. Eden Tigers, meet our new star running back, Blue Bedford." One player after another said "hello Blue." Blue's hands were folded. He looked down at the silver and black soil.

John Jr. stretched his hand out. "I think you are my next door neighbor?" he said. Blue extended his hand. He stepped back and surveyed John Jr. "Are you the son?" he asked.

"Son," John Jr. said.

Big Boy Blue dropped down on the grass. He glared at John Jr. while demonstrating two-hand push-ups, one-hand push-ups, left and right in rapid speed. He jumped up. "The lady," Blue said. "What's her name?"

"My mother?" said John Jr.

Big Boy Blue edged in closer to a raw scar on John Jr.'s forehead. "What's your mother's name?"

"Megan," John Jr. replied.

"That's all I need to know," and he dashed away.

The running track was no match for Blue's strong, long legs. They were fast and fearless. Coach Elmore stared at his watch, and said "Either my watch is broken or his time is real. This guy is unbelievable."

"Coach," Willie interrupted, "why we had to wait two hours for him to come to practice?"

Coach Elmore's head swung, rotated from his watch to Blue. He laughed. "Lateness is the concern of late comers. Willie, if you ran as fast as Blue, you could be late too."

Georgia winter cold resembled a summer cool. It was a rainy season, nevertheless, in November. Coach Elmore was living a dream. In two months, sports newscasters, columnist for the "The Atlanta Constitution" wrote about one player—Blue Bedford. Coach Elmore's status changed from local Atlanta high school coach to an international success. Suddenly college scouts and professional football organizations wanted to be his friend. Blue was making a name for Eden High School; euphoria brand Coach Elmore's heart.

On Friday, before the Regional Championship game, the magnolia trees were pink and purple around two acres of Eden's football field. On the west side, the players performed drills; on the east side were the majorettes; on the north side stood Coach Elmore with his assistant, Leon; and on the South side, Big Boy Blue trained alone.

Sythia twirled her baton high toward the gray and white sky. Savannah flipped hers higher. "Sythia, try this one," she hollered. Savannah's baton dropped down, she swirled twice, the baton popped on her left knee. She grabbed it with her right hand and hurled it back in the air again. Savannah's baton flew back down.

"I bet I can," Sythia said. She jumped in front of Savannah, gripped her baton with her left hand, and held her baton in the right hand. All six majorettes clapped.

"Ladies, enough of show dancing, save your performance for Saturday's game," Mrs. Lockhart said. "I will demonstrate the correct way to control your body, balance your movements like a ballerina, and at the same time, being graceful, athletic like me."

Sythia and Savannah skipped back in the benches, chins pointed directly at Mrs. Lockhart.

Savannah's eyes turned in the direction of the south side. "Just look at him," she whispered. "I may not be a virgin much longer."

"Who?" Sythia asked.

"Sythia, what do you mean 'who'? You keep pretending you don't see him?"

Sythia stared at Mrs. Lockhart. "I try not to look at him. Those Olympian legs could damage your bones."

"Not if you move your legs in the right place," Savannah murmured in Sythia's ear.

Sythia fixed her sight on Mrs. Lockhart. "I thought you and Moe were going together."

"Moe," she stomped her feet. "Moe with the big white teeth? Are you crazy? Besides, my brother Willie said he's been in jail."

"How do you know?" Sythia's hands covered her mouth.

"Sythia, you don't listen. I said Willie told me."

"Oh," she mumbled, and twisted her neck to the south side. "He's handsome, isn't he?"

"I'll take his lips over Moe's teeth anytime." Savannah was silent; four eyes were glued on Big Boy Blue.

Meanwhile, John Jr. and Willie were jumping rope. Willie stopped. He laid his stocky body down in a patch of grass. Coach Elmore spotted him, speedy in seconds above him. "Willie, didn't I tell you to drop off twenty pounds. Get up before I cut you from the team."

"Coach, I was taking a rest, my calves keep cramping on me."

"Hey Coach," Leon, his assistant, yelled, "we got a problem over here."

"I'll be right back, Willie. How many times, have I told you to stretch before and after practice?"

Willie hunkered down on the bench. John Jr. stretched, stared at the majorettes.

"John do you think your Momma will let me come over for dinner tonight?"

"Willie, my Mom said you can't come over every night."

"Who you looking at? I know—Sythia? John, you can forget about her. Daddy is already planning that wedding with Lee Ivy Henderson. They got accepted at Emory University. Why don't you talk to my sister Savannah?"

"Don't Moe and Savannah go together? Moe is telling everybody Savannah is his girl."

"Moe is not going with my sister. Haven't you heard about him?"

Upon his return, Coach Elmore, wailed. "Stand up Willie. Have you ever been in prison?"

"Prison? No, Coach," he said, in a low voice.

"Look at your body. Prison is essentially shortage of space made by a surplus of time."

"Uh, Coach," he snickered.

"I want you to go to the library after practice and read the word prison." Coach Elmore stared at Big Boy Blue who was sprinting at top speed. He left Willie, hurried across the field, calling Blue's name.

"Running our way," Willie said. "There's Moe."

"Where?" John Jr. asked.

"Don't you see big white teeth?"

"Oh yeah," he smiled.

The last game of the year between the Eden Tigers and the Wright Warriors was on December 9, 1972. Great expectations were felt throughout Atlanta football fans. WAOK radio announced, "5,000 tickets were sold for the game at Grady Stadium on Monroe Drive."

Coach Elmore's hands were oily, his heart was optimistic; he tasted a championship ring next year. Big Boy Blue showed no stress. Everyone's eyes were on him. Coach Elmore walked in the team's locker room, "Men remain relaxed, 'cause we got a long night ahead of us." He glanced at Blue, "It's six o'clock and the game starts in one hour. Be confident, courageous tigers." He nodded at Blue, on his way to his private room.

Coach Elmore paced back and forth. His assistant was silent while watching him. He thought about Blue all the time. "Blue is taking my team. If he wanted my job, Principal Reeves would hand it over to him. If we win tonight's game, Blue is guaranteed a top-dog college scholarship. Nobody will remember me." He flopped in a charcoal plastic chair; legs plopped on the worn-out wooden desk. "Blue will be bringing doubts, the same distress to another coach soon. And, even still, Leon I wish we had him three years ago."

"Coach," Leon arms folded, "how did we get him anyway?"

"Principal Reeves said he was going to go pro this year. That was until his high school in Chicago said he was seventeen, ineligible. His mother disputed it, said he was eighteen. She fought with the school officials, showed them Blue's birth certificate. The school heard she was offered some incentives if Blue signed with a team in California. The deal was ready, he changed his mind. His mother shipped him on the midnight train to Georgia the following morning. Rumor has it; he skipped the Chicago Public League Football Championship game in Soldier Field last year, because he disliked his coach."

He stood up, glared at his team from the window. "Look at my players; they don't dare move without looking at Blue. They worship him."

Leon turned his head around, and observed, "Everyone except John Jr., he never looks at Blue."

"And why should he? John Jr. got everything some of these guys don't have—a family and an early acceptance at Morehouse College. He just doesn't care. You know, that kid has heart."

"That kind of heart doesn't make you a superstar," Leon grinned. "Listen to the hollering fans. They don't want Blue's heart. Besides Coach, you will finally get your championship title."

Coach Elmore took his toothpick out of his mouth, "He'll play hard, he'll win, and he'll make lots of money."

"Hell, Coach," Leon laughed, "I say Amen to that."

"Amen ain't got a Damn thing to do with it. It's what my daddy told me when he beat me for stealing a football in a department store on Perry Boulevard. I was twelve, and he said, 'You are a Fearless Stupid Head. You could go to jail. Only a stupid head would steal a football in broad daylight.' Blue might be stupid in the classroom, he's smart on the field. He brought our team this far, through fearless, merciless determination. He knows his hunky head is big, soon to be rich. Nothing is stupid about that."

Blue lay on the wooden bench and began his routine of 300 sit-ups sitting next to John Jr., singing and humming a song, "Baby I'm back." John Jr. looked at Blue. "Hey, do you know this song? My momma in Chicago sang it to me whenever she left me alone to be with her man, except I never wanted her back. What do you think John Jr.?"

"I don't know," John Jr. said, his hand flipping the pages of a *Sports Illustrated Magazine*.

"You don't know what that song means, because you never had a momma like my momma. You a smart boy. I know one thing, if I had a momma that looked like your momma, I would want her to come back."

"Don't talk about my momma," John Jr. tossed the magazine on the floor. Blue smiled and stared at Coach Elmore.

"Blue," Coach Elmore waved for him to come over. "Tonight is a new night for the Eden Tigers team. Our new star, Blue Bedford, has brought us thus far, but not without you. Remember to encourage your teammates." He walked around the room shaking every boy's hand. "I am proud of you," he said. "Now win this game."

The roaring voices of thousands began to chant Blue's name when the Eden Tigers ran on Grady field. In the first quarter, Blue ran a 50-yard dash, and made a touchdown. In the second quarter, he ran a 172 yard touchdown. Not until the third quarter did he run faster than God's eyes could see. He jumped over the Wright Warriors giant defensive backs, and the Eden Tigers won the game to twenty-eight to zero. The stadium roared and rumbled as fans raced on the field. The Eden Tigers had never in their school's history achieved this kind of success. Coach Elmore cherished congratulations from parents, friends, and coaches. News reporters were waiting for interviews with the microphone in Coach Elmore's face. He watched Blue swoosh by and run down to John Jr.

"Hey John Jr., I didn't mean to hurt your feelings earlier. I get like that before the game."

"No problem, you had a great game, Blue." They walked together into the locker room.

"Yeah, thanks. Hey, did your parents come to the game?"

John Jr. opened his locker and grabbed his bag. "No," he slammed the door and walked passed Blue.

"What about Megan?" Blue stood like a Greek God.

John Jr. dropped his bag and zipped his jacket. "My mother doesn't like football." He exited as Coach Elmore entered.

"Blue, what a game, son," Coach Elmore paced back and forth, reciting his statistics. Blue grabbed his towel and headed straight to the shower. He turned the water on steaming hot. "I'm gonna get you, Megan. No son, no husband is gonna stop me"

"Blue, you had a great game, I just want to let you know," the Coach screamed.

"Coach, I can't hear you." He turned the water hotter and placed his head against the wall. His lower legs were spasmodic, his ribs were burning, his mind was thinking of Megan.

3

The half-hour school bell rang at eight thirty-three in the morning. Students boomed through the hallways that Monday. Big Boy Blue carried his Trojan body in a carefree way into his homeroom. He strutted in fifteen minutes late, ignoring the teacher, Mrs. Mansfield, and igniting chatter.

Mrs. Mansfield turned her Masai nose from Big Boy Blue to Mark, who was mumbling incoherently while sleeping. Willie was seated on John Jr.'s left. Blue walked to the back of the room and sat on his right. Chewing his peppermint gum, John Jr. bit his tongue, trying not to scream.

Sunshine gleamed on Blue who glanced at girls passing by the window. He smiled at Diane. "Hello, Blue, you looking mighty fine today." Blue nodded, looked at John Jr. "I know Diane, you won't be getting none today." He nudged John Jr., "How's your mom doing? Man, your mom, Megan, is as fine as she wants to be. Last night, even in the rain, I could smell smothered chicken coming through the walls of my Aunt Rose's home."

Nervously, John Jr. glared in Big Boy Blue's pink and beige eyes. He didn't like the way they made him feel. He remembered seeing the same color last Friday. That's when gossip spread about Ginger and Big Boy Blue in the backseat of her black Camero; rocking and rolling until Principal Reeves spotted them in the parking lot. A burst of laughter erupted when Mrs. Mansfield popped her yellow pencil on Mark's head. "So, John Jr. what is Megan cooking tonight? Sorry I meant to say your mom." Blue said calmly.

"My dad is home, I'm not sure."

"Well yeah, your dad's Mustang is always coming and going Aunt Rose told me." Blue stretched his robust arms behind his thick neck and whispered, "So what's for dinner?"

A ruled notebook dropped on the floor. "I think we're going out to dinner tonight." John Jr. grabbed his book. Instantly, the bell rang, students stumbled out the door.

"See you, Blue." John Jr. jumped over Mrs. Mansfield's shoes, stepping on Sythia's open-toeds.

Blue grasped his number-two pencil and broke it in half. "Yeah," he said.

Dinnertime at the Smith's house was silent. Megan watched her son. "John Jr., what's wrong? You don't look well."

"I'm okay. I hurt my ankle running home from school. I'll ice it down later, Mom." He treaded to his room. Megan cleaned the kitchen. He lay on his Atlanta Falcons pillows, upset that he'd accidentally stepped on Sythia's feet. "Now, she'll never talk to me," he thought. "And...Blue? What's with him?" He cursed his neighbor's name. He ended swimming under the ocean, collapsing, drowning in a nightmare of Blue.

Megan couldn't move off the bed, but her body knew work had to be done, and she had to do it. She gave into her husband's hunger to stop him from begging for another hot morning sunrise. At last he left. She could lie down before washing her son's and husband's shirts. She couldn't wait for another day, because lately every day was empty when she was not with him, Big Boy Blue.

She stepped into her black silk slip, looking at her body in the oval mirror. He could see her from his window; she waited until the wind blew on her face. The white chiffon curtain touched her bare back and wavy hair. She wondered where the wind came from, since it was hot. It seemed like magic flew in and out of her life now with a force of ferocious fire that her body could not stop.

"Good morning Mrs. Smith," Big Boy Blue said. He awoke early, wanting her; hating her every time he heard her and her husband make love. His strong muscles were no match for Megan's lust. She felt powerless, and still she wanted moments of more. He didn't care if she was nineteen years older; he didn't care that he could have every pretty girl at Eden High School; he had something her husband could not provide: permanent love.

"Good morning Big Boy Blue. How are you this beautiful morning? I didn't know you were there. Don't you have school today? John Jr. and my husband left hours ago. It's so hot, and I have lots of housework to do."

Tenderly Blue said, "I'm not going to school today, Mrs. Megan. I could help you around the house or something." Megan grabbed her white silk robe that her had husband brought back from Sweden and slowly tied the loose belt around her svelte waist. She raised her hands, began to maneuver her hair in a French roll. Her voluptuous, vibrant breasts were in sight.

"Oh, that's silly. You can't help me do housework. Besides, I have lots of washing to do. You wouldn't even know how to put detergent in the machine."

Calculating, seizing her desire, he blurted out, "Could I bring over a couple of my shirts too? My Aunt Rose doesn't have a washing machine. If you don't mind, I could drop them off, Mrs. Megan. I will go straight to school, I promise."

She stepped away from the window, then a half a step. "OK, bring your clothes to the basement and I will wash them for you. But you must go to school."

He stared in her clear, cautious eyes, and said, "Uh-huh."

The second homeroom bell rang at ten-thirty o'clock in the morning. John Jr. was as happy as he could be, because Big Boy Blue was late or may have skipped school today. He thought how good it felt not being harassed by Blue's questions about his mother another day.

"Hey John Jr.," Sythia said, "Have you seen Big Boy Blue? He asked me out, and he's not even in school." How could Blue stand her up? he thought. But it was Blue.

"No Sythia, I haven't seen him either."

Synthia turned her head away, and a second later said, "Hey John Jr.... is Megan at home today? Sorry, I meant to say your mother?" She gave John Jr. a girly smile, strutting straight to her chair.

A thunderous lunch bell couldn't match the rush, the roar of his feet running past teachers talking to teachers, boys joking with girls. Books were flying everywhere as John Jr. hit everyone bolting out the front door. He moved faster than Superman, Spiderman, or even Superfly. Son was on a mission to save Mom.

Racing to his house, he looked at Mrs. Rose's house next door and felt crazy about his Mom being with Blue.

"Hey Mom, I'm home, Mom," he said urgently.

"John Jr.," Megan replied, "I'm in the basement washing clothes. I'll be right there. Look in the oven; I cooked your favorite, smothered chicken." John could barely take off his book bag. He curled in the chair eating his chicken. Man, this is my favorite meal. He paused and said, "Blue's too."

He tip-toed down the stairs, his body quivered, his heart, scared. He saw his mom washing someone's clothes—it was Big Boy Blue's blue and gold Tigers football jersey. Megan stopped. She moved away from the washer. Big Boy Blue stretched his towering arms. She embraced his touch.

Woozy knees backtracked to the kitchen. He hunched in the chair, choked tears halted his breath. John Jr. pushed away his no-longer favorite

W. D. Moore

meal. He closed his eyes, contemplated what to do. For it was true—his mom loved Big Boy Blue.

About two hours later, dreamtime terminated when Megan hurried to her son's bedroom. She turned on the light. He dripped in sweat. Still, monstrous screams poured out. "John Jr., wake up. Son, wake up."

He saw his mom. The silk, lavender night robe dragged behind her pink satin slippers, the yellow ribbon tied loosely in a pony tail, dangled below her back, the youthful glow of her skin showed her natural beauty. "Mom, are you all right?" He sat upright, wiping his forehead.

"Me? John Jr., you had a nightmare. What were you dreaming about?"

"I was dreaming," he watched her. "What time is it?"

"It's around one o' clock in the morning. You probably woke the entire neighborhood." She placed her hands on his head. "You don't have a fever. Let me get you a cold glass of water." She attempted to leave his room.

"Mom, when is Dad coming home?"

She held his hand, "Baby, I've been asking your father the same question for eighteen years. He's on a short-tour assignment, and you know what that means by now. I'll be right back. You lie there, and don't go to sleep."

She flowed like a principal ballerina. He stared at her profile. "Mom is pretty," he said: "Dad."

4

Three months ago, Megan saw Blue's eyes. In two months she thought less of her husband. The first Saturday in December, she slept late to escape. "One minute the sky is dry, the next hour it rains. I've never heard of this much rain in Atlanta." Megan turned over, lifted her head from the cover. "I'll try to clean my back yard before thunder begins. If I'm lucky, I can remove the dead branches fallen off the Willow tree."

She slipped into black dungaree pants and black sweater and strolled to her son's room. She knocked on the door, "John Jr., wake up, and help your mom in the yard." There was no answer. She waited and thought about their conversation last night.

"I may quit the team," he said. "Coach don't need me anyhow, 'cause they got a star." He stormed in the family room to watch basketball on television. The star, Megan didn't ask, since she knew it was Big Boy Blue. He was in all the newspapers, the talk of Georgia. She kept the window shade down.

"No more games," she thought. "I have a family. I've been bored. When my husband comes home, I won't even think about my neighbor." She knocked harder, shoved the door open. He was not there. A white piece of paper lay on his unmade bed.

"Mom, I am going to the movies with Willie to catch the $1.00 special at noon. We have to get there early before there are no more seats. I didn't want to wake you. See you later for dinner. Oh, yeah, Mom, I invited Willie."

Ripping the paper, she hollered, "How many times have I told you to ask me before you tell me? He never listens to me. I'm raising a son by myself. I might as well get used to it."

She charged to the basement. "The wind will not stop me today, I'll move the branches and clean the yard, myself," she said, while stepping into her white rubber boots, grabbing her handy gloves. The bristling wind blew leaves in the air. She hauled branches into her two-wheeled barrow. She held a main stem of a willow tree. The burst of the wind pushed her body off balance. She stumbled, fell hard on the ground. "Darn it," she screamed. Seconds later lighting erupted, wind bursting-swooshing her skin, hair twisting in her face. At that moment, she heard a voice. She was holding onto the willow tree.

"Mrs. Smith, let me help you." Big Boy Blue picked her up. The garage door swung open. She held onto his steel neck. He gently released her. The rain pounced at the door. He locked it. He looked at the leaves in her hair, the wetness of her body. His hand carefully removed leaves from her face and he pushed her hair back behind her ears. Softly he said, "We should stay here until the rain stops. I don't want you to get hurt, Megan." She remained silent. She stared at his large, muscular arms, the wet, white Eden Tigers tee shirt. "I hope you don't mind that I called you Megan." He looked at her mouth, she at his, and he drew her closer to him. She rested her misty eyes on his broad shoulders. He lifted her chin, "I want to kiss you Megan," he whispered, "but I won't, not now. I'll let you decide when I can."

She withdrew from him. "You are asking me?" she whispered.

He pulled her in closer, wiped the tears off her face. "Yes, I'm asking." He moved his lips toward hers.

"You better leave before my son comes home." She staggered away from him.

"I'll leave, because I know you want me to stay." He opened the garage door, the wind pounding on his face. He held it for a minute, and she watched his strength. Her hair blew in the wind. Their minds sensed each other's will.

"Blue, thank you for helping me outside," she uttered. He stared at her wet sweater. "Megan, you could catch a cold. I'll call you later. You can let me know."

"Let you know what?"

"If I can come."

"You have my number?" She stepped backward.

"Yes," he waved goodbye.

"I should lock the door," she thought. She sauntered into her kitchen and suddenly, ran to her bedroom.

In a few minutes Blue was in his room, lounging on the twin bed—desiring Megan. He knew today he would have her. He remembered, Lulu lying down on his momma's bed, "Why don't you enjoy it and enjoy until the next time." Lulu was thirty-six and Blue was sixteen. She seduced him on his birthday, and every day, until one day she said "no." Three days later she came back and taught him some more.

Blue would never forget Lulu's words, "Blue Baby, this is our secret. Don't tell your momma." The very last time, Lulu said "Blue, I can't see you no "mo." Boy I done taught you too good." Lulu gave it to him again, and said, "I feel sorry for any woman who loves you, 'cause you got something special." She looked down at his skillful hands, "I ain't talking about the obvious," and closed the door.

That was two years ago. Now Blue is eighteen and eager for Megan's body.

He saw Megan two months before she noticed him. He watched her as the heavy breeze blurred across her lovely face while she brushed her hair. He first thought that she was a young girl, until he heard her voice speaking to a man of lust. The pleasure of the man's passion brought pain to his body because he desired more. When she finished with him, she stood, went to the window, and let the wind blow through her wet hair.

Blue's heart was pumping as he prepared his words while lying in his single bed dreaming about meeting Megan. The following Sunday, he saw her alone, sitting outside on her back porch. His hands were sweating, his mouth was sensing, his body was strong. Except while walking closer, he felt weak. And when he walked away, she said "What did you say your name was?" He knew they would be together.

But for Megan, time changed. How could she stop the train when her body wanted Big Boy Blue? She had never been with another man, and now she felt Blue. She raced into the shower to think things through. She heard the telephone ring; she pretended it was not him.

"Hello," she said. Water dripped everywhere.

The rain continued to beat at Megan's window—but no matter—the steam in her shower was stronger when Blue and she made love.

And so, silent and still, they lay in her bed. He told her how his father was a top sprinter in Chicago. "I watched him since I was three years old," Blue said. "My father taught me how to train. His speed was ten times greater than mine. He had discipline, determination. I owe my power to him."

"What about your mother?" she asked.

"My will, every bone in my body to win, that would be my mother."

She listened. He loved her until she made him go home. He came back the next morning. She learned about football, he learned how to touch, talk, and take care of Megan.

In Spain it was crisp and cold. John had been stationed at the Morón Air Base, thirty-five miles southeast of Seville. This short tour turned into three-month one. He was scheduled to fly back to the states the following day. It appeared that American service men were plenty, taking in the sights. He easily felt comfortable, and yet his mind went back home to his wife.

"I tried telephoning the house last night, and there was no answer. She is purposely not answering the phone," he said to his co-pilot. "She knows I'm calling, care for her, more than life. Why does she torment me so?"

They sat at Café Seville, looking out at the snow, eating steak and lamb. "Captain," Fat Mitch said, "women, don't have nothing to do but torment us. Why else would they make us wait to love them, and then when we do, they treat us like fools?" He savaged his second order of lamb shanks, sprinkled two teaspoons of salt on his meat, and drank a bottle of Caña beer. He winked at the waitress. "I ain't ever going back to the states, when I can eat great food like this, and that's not all I'm talking about."

A half glass of sherry wine was in John's glass. He said "You say the same words in every country we land. You don't change, just your stomach."

"They don't call me Fat Mitch from Detroit cause of my stomach. Even at Lewis College the guys knew; I like myself some fat, thick thighs, and man I see a lot of them here." He chuckled with a mouth full of cannellini beans.

"Exactly," said John. "You see thighs everywhere you go."

"Well, at least I'm getting some. You don't look at any legs, any shape. Why? 'Cause you got a woman on your mind that you can't get on the phone."

John waved to the waitress, pointed to his glass. His posture upright; his fist closed tight. With might he said, "I got a wife, a woman. There is a difference between eating different pieces of chicken every night: You got to train her, tame her each time, and without money, you don't get no honey, so shut the fuck up."

Captain Fat Mitch laughed, remained quiet. His sharp knife cut away, staring out at the window. A thin brunette woman strolled by. "She's too skinny for me, cute though, very cute. One night, you gonna call your wife, she won't answer the phone, that sexy thing there is gonna give you what your wife can't. And you gonna take it, 'cause no matter how much you love your woman, she ain't here."

Abraham Lincoln bills dropped on the table. John straightened his hat and swallowed his wine. Politely he said, "You just a fool Fat Mitch. I've been a fighter pilot for over twenty years. I have never had a stupid fool like you for a partner. It serves me right, for joining back up when I did. Whatever you eat tonight, hope you make it back to the base, on time. I won't be delayed, waiting for your late ass." John scurried passed customers coming in Café Seville. He muttered, "No more calling you Baby, I'll see you tomorrow."

There was a brilliant blue kind of day on Chester Street. When her son left for school, Big Boy Blue entered through the basement door. He caressed her wavy hair, kissed her warm lips. "Baby, I can't breathe," Megan said.

"I can't breathe whenever I am not with you." He longed for her once more. Afterwards they showered and he dressed. Walking down the staircase, they held hands. At the patio door, his arms clinched her waist. Her palms massaged his neck. "I'll see you tomorrow," said Blue, who kissed her promptly. He stared in her bright eyes. "Good morning," he whispered. She smiled.

In the kitchen, she brewed dark Guatemalan coffee, John's favorite. "Am I falling in love with Blue?" With wonderment, she said, "I love my husband, but I feel something special for Blue." While in her thoughts, she did not hear the first ring. It rang again, she blocked it out. Coffee mug in her hand, she trudged to her bedroom and relaxed in her vanity chair, looking at the Willow tree. "I'm daydreaming, when I have housework to do." Real time surfaced when she glanced at the bed. Her duties began. She changed the linen and cleaned the bathroom. A half hour later, she cleaned John Jr.'s room, lugging his dirty clothes to the laundry room, tiding his bed, collecting college catalogs and magazines off the floor. "What is John Jr. doing with this?" She asked abruptly, throwing the West Point Military Academy brochure in the garbage basket.

She trailed to her closet, dressed in a pleated, purple skirt, pink wool sweater, and suede heels. With a leather purse on her shoulders, she entered the kitchen. As soon as she peeked in the refrigerator, she uttered, "There's no food in the house. I've been busy with Blue. I forgot to go food shopping." She grabbed her raincoat and car keys and opened the door. "John," she said. He held her firm, "Baby, I can't breathe," she said.

With luggage in one hand, he gripped her hand with the other. "Where are you going? Why haven't you been answering the phone?" He dropped his United States Air Force bag and tossed his grey wool coat in the armchair. She withdrew from him and cast her J. Riggin's coat over his. Exasperated, she explained, "John, I'm sorry. I didn't want you to hear the same story; you were not coming home."

He relaxed his back on the canvas sofa, reaching for her hands. She came to him. She rubbed his trimmed, salt-and-pepper hair. His arms were wrapped around her smooth legs. "Baby, don't torment me like that again," he said and unzipped her skirt.

"John, right now, Baby, I was on my way to the grocery store."

"Come on Baby," he said, softly. She sat on his lap; he unbuttoned her sweater and unsnapped her lace bra. "I need you. I missed you so much. I may resign from the reserve."

All of a sudden, she snatched her body from him. His grip caught her hand. "Do you really mean it this time? Will you resign?" she asked, tears gliding down.

He brought her body back to him and laid her gently on the sofa. "You have the most beautiful body. You don't know what it's like wanting you. My heart is hopeless without you." His tender kisses dried her weepy eyes. He removed her black sheer panties.

Megan moaned, "John." He moved inside, she with him.

At Eden High School, there was a different kind of motion when Blue sailed into Mrs. Bertha Henry's homeroom class. She was grading papers, blurted out, "Young man, you are late. This is the last time you will be allowed in my classroom without a permit from the principal's office."

Sythia glared. Savannah giggled and said, "Hey Blue." He turned his head to John Jr. in the back row. Mrs. Henry launched toward Savannah, "You have an assignment, young lady. Don't interrupt me while I am speaking." She pointed her number-two pencil at Blue. "This is the last time you will be allowed in my room late, Mr. Blue Bedford."

He gazed at Sythia, "Sythia, you look like a ripe peach, not spoiled like your friend, Savannah." The entire class rose to laughter. John Jr. and Willie were not amused. Blue's moonless eyes penetrated John Jr., modest eyes. He wandered to a chair next to him. "Say, John Jr., Coach Elmore mentioned you quitting the team. I guess you might as well, since you can't even throw a tennis ball."

Willie intercepted, "John Jr. is second-in-line quarterback for the team."

His grimaced, shifted to Willie, "How did you become a defensive guard when your overweight body can't guard yourself." He walked to the front and stopped at Savannah's desk. "Your brother is a balloon ready to burst. What about you, Savannah?"

Flustered, Savannah faked a snigger. Mrs. Henry approached Blue. "Mr. Bedford, leave my room—go to the principal's office this minute. I will not have you disrupting my class any longer."

"I'm right behind you Mrs. Henry." Blue said. He followed her marching flat heels out of the classroom.

Willie whispered to John Jr., "Why does he hate you? He's always speaking down at you. I think it's because you're smart, he's a stupid superstar at our school. He acts like he runs Eden High. Everybody treats him like he is, except for Mrs. Henry."

"I don't care; I'll be in college next year. Who cares about football, anyway?"

"What? You love playing as much as I do." Willie watched his sister, Savannah.

"Yeah, I know." John Jr. stared at Sythia.

Outside the principal's office, Mrs. Henry entered without knocking. "Principal Reeves, Blue Bedford is late every day. He disrupts my class whenever he's there. I am told he is failing other classes and reports to class at his discretion. However, he attends football practice. Coach Elmore allows him to treat the gym like his personal castle. Who is the principal at Eden? Blue Belford should be disciplined, or talked to about the guidelines of graduating from high school."

With a never-ending twitched in his left eye, Principal Reeves' chair twisted away from her. He stared at Big Boy Blue. But moments afterwards, he twirled out of his seat to face her. "I am the principal at Eden High. Please do not assume I am unaware of my students at our school. Now, I will speak to you later about the situation. In the meantime, your students are waiting for you in class, Mrs. Henry." With a twinkle in his eye, he said, "Blue Bedford, please have a seat.

Aggravated, Mrs. Henry said, "I want to talk about this student—I will not be disrespected."

"Bertha, I am not disrespecting you, I prefer to speak to the student first. Will you calm down? I promise we shall have our talk shortly."

"And I don't care if Eden wins a championship title." She sighed at the sight of Blue. The door knob clanged harder than a slammed home run by George Herman Ruth.

"His eye stopped twitching, when she left the room," Blue thought. He smiled.

"Blue, this morning, I spoke to WSB sports radio about interviewing you. The story line will focus on Eden's journey to our first regional title. I don't have to tell you what it has meant to have you here. Coach Elmore is proud of you, and of course, none of Eden's accomplishments this year would have been possible without your presence on the team. As for, Mrs. Henry, well, she is a nice lady. It's too bad she is retiring next spring. Could you cooperate with her, come to her class on time? We will work with your grades. Your graduating status is guaranteed. Remember our agreement, son. Besides, your dreams of playing professional football are almost here."

He leaned his powerful physique on the door. "Principal Reeves, I can leave or stay. Either way, I am going to play pro ball. You tell Bertha to get in line before I walk out of Eden and transfer to Valdosta." Principal Reeves's slight shoulders were erect; he popped up in his black executive chair. "Mrs. Henry does not understand high-level politics. You are bringing great interest to Eden and revenue to the community. She is a strict disciplinarian who has developed top academic scholarships for our students. Don't worry about Mrs. Henry. We are fortunate you brought your talents to Eden High School. I want you to come to me with any future concerns."

"I feel sick," Blue thought. "The entire village of Eden High is suffocating me." His hands leaned on Principal Reeves' desk. "I need to use your telephone."

"My phone? What's wrong with the telephone in the hallway?"

Blue's muscular arms leaned in closer. Principal Reeves' eye twitched. "I want to make a personal call," he commanded. "Or, should I sprint to Lakeside and ask them?"

"That's fine, of course you can telephone your family, go right ahead." Principal Reeves stepped aside from his desk and galloped to the door. "No problem. I have a meeting with Mrs. Henry." To his secretary, he said, "Blue Bedford is authorized to use my telephone. I will be right back."

In Principal Reeve's colossal chair, Blue was a Chadian Prince. He dialed her number.

Asleep, John rested on the sofa. Megan covered his jetlagged body with a soft-cozy knitted throw. She hung his coat in the closet, removed his Oxford shoes, and unpacked his luggage. The living room lights were dimmed. She headed to the kitchen. "What am I going to cook for dinner?" She saw a frozen whole chicken, and as she ran water, the telephone rang. "Hello," she said.

"Baby, I need to see you, I'm coming over now."

Her restrained speech was different from the terror in her heart. "Blue, my husband is home. I can't talk to you, see you, or be with you. Don't try to see me, and please, never stop by." She hung up the phone and switched the volume off. She tip-toed over to her husband; he was still sleeping peacefully. Megan returned to the kitchen. The cold water was gushing, running on the floor. Her heart was harder than the chicken. She turned the water off and tossed the chicken in the freezer. Her body froze. She braced for an anxiety attack. Screaming inside her mind, "Dear God, what am I going to do."

Blue redialed Megan's number. He banged the phone and stormed out of Principal Reeves's office. Fast, his legs lunged to the football field. He sprinted north, south, and a mile around the track. He lost his breathe and stopped. He waited for thirty seconds, back-tracked south, north, for two miles. Coach Elmore watched him and timed him on his speedometer. When he could no longer move his body, he ripped off his wet tee shirt and stretched his body on the sticky grass. His eyes glared at the burning sun; his heart was exploding like a pipe bomb; his lungs screamed farther than Mercury and Venus; his heart screeched inside his soul, "Megan, I can't breathe."

A huffing and puffing, Coach Elmore's hat blew to the ground as he darted to Blue. "What's wrong? What happened? Do you know you surpassed your record by 40 seconds?" Coach Elmore asked. He jumped for joy and chortle to himself.

"What the fuck do I care," Blue said. "I can turn it on and off whenever I want to. What do you think I am, your servant? I am a student, a senior, and nobody's meal ticket. You best hope, I don't leave Eden before you get your damn championship ring."

Frightened eyes observed Blue's exit. Coach Elmore began rubbing, his wedding band. "I'm losing weight worrying about this fool and my fate. It's only a championship title I have wanted all my life. I know I am close, but I can't eat or sleep thinking about what he will do tomorrow." Rushing into the gym, he said, "Bedford will be okay, and I'll get my ring."

The water in the men's shower room was on. Coach Elmore yelled, "Hey Blue, remember, you're in the Six Flags Over Georgia's football passing contest Sunday." In his thoughts, he murmured, "I can see it now: Eden High named one of the Top Ten teams in Georgia by UPI's twenty-four member Coaches' Board."

5

Two days elapsed. Blue said, "Her husband will leave again, and I will be in Megan's bed. I never cared for anybody like her, not even my father and never my mother. I do like Megan in a real good way. It's time. I need to see her." He lingered in the gym working on his strength routine.

His body was in perfect condition. He admired his physique and uttered, "I got what she wants and I'm gonna give it to her. She can use me. I don't care, as long as I can have her. My daddy told me about women. Yeah, he told me when I was ten years old who my momma was. I'll never forgive her for killing my baby sister. She doesn't know I know, but my daddy told me what she did when I was sixteen.

He said "Blue, your momma, Bonnie, was a good-looking woman. I was running track; she ran my mind. I gave up my dream to win a gold medal to be with her. I stopped training after you were born. She stopped letting me love her. She stayed out every night. I told her I was leaving."

"Good," she said. "But if you do, I'm gonna get rid of our new baby. I'm pregnant."

I would not leave you. I watched your momma grow bigger by the day. At six months she said "I don't want this baby inside of me. I'm gonna kill myself if I have this baby. I got to get this baby out of me."

We went to the doctor. The doctor said "There's nothing you can do about it. You are six months pregnant, Mrs. Bedford."

"You take this baby out of me, or I will." The doctor asked us to leave. Tears rolled down your momma's face. She said "I'm gonna kill myself if you don't do something."

"I will not," I told her. She ran, left me outside the doctor's office. That night she didn't come home.

The following night she telephoned, "I feel better. I'm staying at Bessie's house for few days."

She was nice, sweet like she used to be. I loved her. Four more days went by. I came home from work. Bonnie was joking around with Frankie from Black Belt Chicago. They were drinking Johnnie Walker.

"Frankie came over for a visit to see how I was doing," she said.

"Where is my baby?" I asked? She looked at Frankie.

"There ain't no baby," he said.

I dropped down, cried for my child.

"It wasn't your baby anyway, Bernard, so what you crying about?"

She and Frankie continued talking. When the whisky was gone, she told Frankie to leave.

"Man, you a fool," he said, stumbling over me.

"How could you?" I yelled. You were in the kitchen doing your homework. She said, "Blue baby, your momma and dad got our work to do. Go to your bedroom."

"I know what's wrong with you, Bernard," she said. "You ain't had my loving for long time. She wore a red slip and stretched her legs on the daybed. Little by little, she lifted her slip. "Come on over here, Bernard." I came but stopped when I saw dark, butchered scars across her stomach.

Uncontrollable chuckling emerged. She said, "It will heal in a few weeks."

"I'm leaving and taking Blue with me." She stormed toward your room.

"You can leave right now, but not with my son."

I didn't ask what she meant, my bags were already packed. I just didn't know."

At evening time at Eden, Big Boy Blue zipped his jacket and switched the lights out in the gym. He was hungry and wanted Megan's sweet potato pie. "I think I'll go over there, ask for a piece, and see if she can sneak a little bit on the side."

Dinner time at the Smith's, John unlocked his black leather brief case. He rolled up his white cotton shirt, reviewed their Coca-Cola and Georgia Pacific bonds, bank checking account and investment accounts at First National Bank of Atlanta. He wrote out checks: mortgage, utilities, car notes, credit cards, and monthly expenses for Megan. Retirement, savings, and John Jr.'s college were at Citizen Trust Bank. He made a note to call the bank about the dividends accrued from his inheritance. "I need to call Mom and Dad to make sure they like their new live-in attendant," John said. He opened their mahogany secretary desk and looked for stamps.

"Supper will be ready in five minutes boys." Megan strolled in next to John and kissed his cheeks.

"Mom, can Willie eat with us tonight?" John Jr. popped his head in his parents' bedroom.

"John Jr., Willie can't eat with us every night." She said sharply. "Sweetheart, your father's home. Let it just be family tonight."

"Okay, Mom, I'll tell him, he's holding on the phone."

She grinned. She stared at her husband, blew a kiss in his direction. Her toned legs turned. John said, "I'll be right down Baby. Is it a special dinner baby? You look pretty enough to eat?" She smiled and swirled down stairs.

With the papers were filed and locked. John strode to his son's room. "Hey, what's this sulking for? You know your momma likes her two men around. Make sure you mention how pretty she looks, and Willie can come over tomorrow night." They chuckled.

"Dad, are you going to be home for a while now? Mom really misses you."

"I know son, and I miss both of you. My career takes me from my family, but I always return. The Air Force Reserve keeps my family well-provided for, expenses are increasing, and college bills will be high, whether or not you received a full scholarship. I have to plan for my family's future. Listen, I'm retiring in another year. You will be in college and your mom and I will be bored together at home until we have grandchildren."

"Dad, be real, that's ages from here."

"You think so? Time creeps up. Look at you. You're almost taller than your dad. John Jr. was quiet, holding his football.

"Looks like your team is headed to win a championship. Who would have ever expected that?" John patted him on the back. "Hey, I'm home. I can go to your games."

"I'm going to quit." John Jr. threw his football in the laundry basket.

"Quit? Why would you say such nonsense?" John retrieved the ball and tossed it to John Jr.

"You are a first-rate quarterback. What's going on?"

"Dad, it's not fun like before, and besides, Coach Elmore don't let me play anymore. He's wrapped around his new running back, and nothing else matters to him. He called me in his office to reassure me I would play. Except he said I'm a smart college boy, what do I need football for?"

"Son, I don't care what your coach said. You like football, and you can play football. You deserve to play. You're dedicated to the game, and your grades. You love the game; as you grow older, you will appreciate having another outlet in your life. But for now, don't quit the team."

"Dad, I want to ask you something."

"Yes, son, I'm here."

"The ROTC counselor asked me if I was interested in West Point Military Academy."

"He what!" he said. "When, and what brought this on?"

"Well, I told him you were a Captain in the Air Force, a fighter pilot. He was impressed, and he leaped from his seat. He went on about how difficult it is to be a fighter pilot, and how much he wanted to meet you."

"That's nice, son, but, what did you say?"

"I said I was interested, and that I always wanted to be like my Dad."

"John Jr., you never once mentioned your interest in a career in the military. Morehouse has been the name in our home since you were seven years old."

"Dad, I know, but, I never wanted to go to Morehouse. Mom wants me to. And I said okay."

"I didn't raise you to be afraid. However, if you are serious, then you got to jump on it right away."

"I sorta have, Dad."

John folded his arms and his eyes lit like a flashlight. "What did you do, son."

"I applied over six months ago, and I think I might get in. I should know by January. I need a nomination from you. I wanted to ask you about it."

"Son, this is what happens when a father stays on tours. He finds his son is grown."

"Dad, I'm seventeen." "I know, son."

"What did your mother say?"

"I haven't mentioned it to her, at least until I get accepted."

"I'll contact West Point about the cadet vacancies, and you must prepare the words for your mother. You are a grown man."

"Yes, Dad, I will." John Jr. hugged his Dad, his Dad hustled the ball away from his hands. His son retrieved the ball. John nodded, popped him on the head.

Megan's roasted turkey, simmered in rosemary, red onions, and cornbread stuffing seeped into every part of the house. John said, "Your mother is killing me, son, let's go down stairs for dinner."

A knife in her hands, she chopped a chuck of sweet South Carolina butter in the mashed potatoes. "It needs a little bit more salt," she thought to herself.

Staring at Mrs. Rose's house, she took off her apron. "It's over. I refuse to think about Blue." She set baby green peas on the table. "I can't have him," she sighed.

He tip-toped behind her, pulled his arms around her waist. "It smells good in here, and I'm not talking about the turkey." She turned around and hugged her husband.

"Mom, you look pretty," John Jr. quickly said. "Hey, where are the biscuits?"

"Biscuits? Oh, they are in the oven," she said. "Darn it, they are burnt."

"Baby, burnt is the way I like it." John replied, kissed her on the cheeks.

"Me too, Mom. You sure look nice today," John Jr. said hurriedly. "Mom where is the butter?"

"On the table John Jr.," she paused, prayed, "Heavenly father; thank you for this meal, we are grateful to be here as a family. Amen."

John Jr. grabbed two biscuits. "Mom, can I save two biscuits for Willie. He won't mind if they are burnt either."

She watched John slice the dark meat for himself, the white meat for her and John Jr. "Willie can come to dinner tomorrow, John Jr." Father and son grinned and she giggled.

After dinner, John Jr. asked, "Mom, what's for dessert? Please say its sweet potato pie?"

"No, John Jr., there is only one slice of pie left. I saved it for your father. Vanilla ice cream is your dessert."

"Ice cream and no pie?"

"And, John Jr., who ate the entire pie?" She walked over to the china cabinet. "You and Willie. The last slice goes to your father. I'll bake two pies on Sunday. Do you want ice cream or not?"

"Yes, Mom. Can I eat it in my room?" John Jr. looked at his Dad.

"No," she answered.

"Dad?"

Her husband patted her behind. "Baby this one time," John smiled—and suddenly, kissed her lips.

The doorbell rang. "Okay," she said softly, removing dishes from the table. "See who is at the door. It better not be Willie, John Jr."

It felt as if a quiet, quick storm was in the air. John Jr. was shocked, silent for several seconds. Megan sensed something Blue.

"Son," John asked, "who is at the door?" He walked to the living room. Big Boy Blue entered. John stood beside his son.

"Good evening, everybody," Blue said, "Sir, my name is Blue Bedford. I'm Mrs. Rose's nephew. I came over to talk to John Jr."

"Hey, aren't you the star running back I've been reading about in the papers?" John remarked, reached out his hand to Blue. "Come on in son, I heard you were staying with your Aunt Rose. How is she doing? We think of her as family, you know. I've been busy these few days, but make sure you tell her I'll be over to see her this weekend." Blue's eyes crossed to the kitchen. John Jr. fixed on Blue. "Megan, we have company."

"I'm cleaning the kitchen," she somberly said. "I'll be right out."

"Have a seat, Blue. We finished dinner, but would you like a soda or something?" John sat on the cushy sofa; Blue's eyes returned the piercing look from John Jr.

"No sir," Blue said politely. I only stopped by because Coach Elmore asked me to check in on John Jr. Coach mentioned he quit the team. He's concerned, because John Jr. is his main back-up quarterback. He knows we are neighbors, and I offered to try to convince John Jr. to stay on the team. Especially, since the team's goal is the state championship title next year."

There was dead silence. John Jr. never left Blue's gaze until his father said, "We were talking about football earlier, and my son is on the team. John Jr. did you actually quit, son?"

Quick-tempered, John Jr. moved closer to Blue. "I told Coach Elmore I might be quitting the team." He put his hands on the door knob. "You didn't have to come by." Blue was silent.

An agitated John interrupted, "John Jr., I want to talk to you—in your room."

"But, Dad, it's not true. I'm staying on the team." He watched his father bolt. Blue remained still.

"John Jr.," John screamed.

Megan entered, her hands crossed behind her waist. She looked at her son run up the staircase. Hurriedly, she reversed her sandals to the kitchen.

Cautiously, she waited. Carefully, he sauntered in. She rested her body in front of the sink. He stood close. "Hello, Megan."

"Hello, Blue," she whispered.

White Adidas sneakers brushed white Dr. Scholl's sandals. "I miss you," Blue softly said.

She staggered to the wood tray and wrapped a slice of sweet potato pie in foil paper. "This is all I can give you Blue." She said delicately, her fingers caressed his hand.

He grabbed her rose-painted nails, kissed her palm. "Good night," he whispered, before exiting by the kitchen door. She watched him through the window. He waved, she waved back.

"Why did I do that?" she said loudly.

"Why did you do what?" John asked.

"What?"

"Nothing," he mumbled, opening the refrigerator door. "That's settled. John Jr. will not quit the team. He's acting a bit jealous of the star next door. I told him: Don't compare yourself to anybody."

"I'm glad," Megan uttered, wiping the countertop table.

"Baby, where is the pie? I don't see it."

"Pie?" She echoed. "There's no more pie."

Bewildered, John said, "Baby, you said there was one slice left."

"John, I'm tired. Could I finish my work down here? I'll be right upstairs." She placed left over gravy in a Tupperware bowl.

Several long minutes, he lay in bed; his legs were wide underneath the pressed white sheets. His baseball arms held both pillows. In a short minute, Megan strolled in the bedroom and unbuttoned her navy sweater dress.

"I forgot to put panties on today," she said playfully.

"Come here." Her stoic body was still. He snatched her to their bed.

"You mean you had no panties on at dinner?" He unclasped her silver hair clip; rumpled waves hung on his bare chest. "Baby," he cried, turning the Tiffany lamp off. Her burning eyes faced the window, the chiffon curtains were blowing in the wind. She wanted him. Her heart was beating, her body was yearning, and her mind was speaking Big Boy Blue. She gave her husband what he hungered for, and he moaned. "Megan."

6

Three days before Christmas 1972, John had been home with his family for two weeks. Life was good. He decided to surprise Megan with the biggest Christmas tree from the Atlanta State Farmers Market in Forest Park. John Jr. was happy because he passed his driver's license exam. He drove his dad's hot red Mustang.

As she was rearranging furniture to make space for the Christmas tree, Megan heard the car. She looked through the window; it was Big Boy Blue's Nova, and a young girl. They were laughing. "I don't care," Megan said, "He should date." She turned the radio on, moved boxes, wrapping paper, ribbons, and presents to the dining room table. She carried a box of old Christmas lights, decorations to be cleaned in the kitchen. She peeked at Blue's car, placed everything on the table. Quickly she ran to her bedroom and slowly laid her head on the bed. "He is torturing me tonight the way I torture him every night." She wiped her eyes. "John will be here with our tree soon." She heard a 'boom.' Megan's heart jumped. A rattling, roaring sound came from the basement. "The dryer," she said. Dashing to the basement the radio was blasting, The Four Tops, "Baby, I Need Your Loving…Got to have all your loving."

"No, not really," she screamed, "I need a new washing machine." The door was open; wet clothes scattered on the floor. "This is just too much. I don't understand why John refuses to buy a new washer." Grabbing her clothes, she tossed them back into the washer. She heard a knock at the basement door. "John, really. Use your key," she yelled, trotting to open the door.

A harder knock, "I don't have a key," he said. Blue walked in.

"Blue, what are you doing here? My husband will be here soon." Lowering her voice, she asked, "Don't you have company?" Wet lingerie in her hands, she bustled to the dryer.

"I do. She's talking to my aunt." He moved in closer.

"Don't you think you should go back to your girl friend?" She murmured bristly.

He grasped her waist, caressed her back, and his head lean down upon her tangerine shirt. She turned to face him, and touched his neck. They kissed, ceasing for moments to gaze in the other's eyes. "I think I love you," he said, whispering in her ear. And in the next moment, he was gone.

Soundless, she said, "I think I'm falling in love with Blue." She tossed the wet clothes in the dryer. The washing machine rumbled. She skipped from the basement and entered the kitchen.

"Mom, we got the biggest Christmas tree, wait to you see it. Dad even let me drive with the sunroof down."

Megan listened to the radio. The Four Tops, "I Can't Help Myself (Sugar Pie, Honeybunch)."

Blue returned home to find Savannah and his Aunt Rose drinking Coca-Cola. "Blue, where have you been, boy? I'm tired, and this young lady got to go to home, and I need to go to bed. Be careful driving with all those Christmas shoppers. My Nova may be an old car, but it is the only car I have."

"It was nice meeting you Mrs. Rose," Savannah said.

A wooden cane in her hand, she replied. "Well, I hope to see you another time. I enjoyed our conversation."

"Aunt Rose," Blue said hurriedly, "I'll turn the lights out and lock the doors before I go to bed."

"Don't stay out too late, Blue," she added, "tomorrow is the last day of school, and you should try to be on time."

With hands on her hips and mouth extended wide, Savannah said abruptly, "Blue, what happened to you? You bring me here; leave me, and now you taking me home. Where did you go?"

Car keys dangling in one hand, he grabbed her wrist with the other. "Let's go, before you get in trouble." Backing out of his driveway, he frowned at John and John Jr. hauling a Christmas tree in Megan's home.

"Trouble, that's why I came over," Savannah's swaggering voice said. "I was hoping for trouble."

He drove to Simpson Street two blocks from her home and parked his car in front of a vacant lot. "Blue, why are you stopping here?" she asked.

His downcast eyes were transfixed to the black sky. "I thought you said you wanted trouble." He turned the car off. "Get in the back seat." Aloof, he said.

"No, I won't," she returned.

"Fine, I'll take you home then." He speeded, and dropped her off at her house.

She stared at Blue. "Blue, you won't tell anybody, will you?"

He placed his majestic hand on her majorettes' leg. "Why would I tell anyone? I like you," he said, turning the car around, he drove to the first vacant lot. She directed her white boots to the back seat. Thirty minutes later, he charged his car, chasing the green light to bring her home. Savannah let herself out. "You're not a virgin now. Next time, it won't hurt," Blue said.

Savannah's shaky body walked to his window, fragile hands touched his steering wheel. Tears flowed down her young girl's face. "Will there be a next time, Blue?" She asked sweetly.

"No," sourly he returned. "I don't like you that much." Brand new Michelin tires accelerated to the slippery I-75 highway.

The next day, Savannah's pain was worst than severe cramps. She headed to her French class and saw her best friend, Sythia, waiting for her. "Thank God, today is the last day of school." Sythia said, and after a long pause. "Hey, let's go over to Lenox Square Mall. We can pretend were not buying each other's Christmas presents. My boyfriend will take us." Savannah hinged as Blue approached.

"Hey Blue."

He did not look at her or speak to her, instead he said, "Hey Sythia." Blue held a football in his hand; his teammates trailed behind. He hustled down the hallway.

"Why did he speak to you?" Savannah said loudly. "Are you seeing him or something?"

"No," Sythia said softly. "What's wrong with you? Why are you upset? You know Ivy is my boyfriend." Mistiness enveloped her eyes; Savannah walked in their class and sat down. She rolled her eyes at Sythia. She whispered in her ear, "You better not be seeing him." Sythia read her vocabulary words; Savannah turned her book over. When the bell rang, Savannah stayed seated. Everyone ran out the door. "Merry Christmas," Sythia said. "Call me if you want to talk."

Still sitting at her desk, Savannah placed her head on her French Literature book, folded her arms around her face, cried and cursed the name, Big Boy Blue.

Outside, Eden High students and teachers were saying good-bye, Merry Christmas, celebrating the start of the holiday. Excluding Willie, who was finishing his test in American History. John Jr. waited for Willie in front of building. Ten minutes passed, Willie said, "I'm finished John Jr., let's go."

"How did you do Willie? Do you think you passed the class? John Jr. said, throwing his football in the air.

"I don't think so John Jr., I'm not smart like you. I'll be lucky, if I get accepted in a four-year college. I may have to attend DeKalb Community College to bring my grades above average. Mrs. Henry said then I can apply at Atlanta University."

"Willie, you will pass. Why don't you apply at Morris Brown College—just in case?"

"Yeah," Maybe, I'll talk to Mrs. Henry about it." Willie's head swerved at the yellow Corvette. "Look is that Sythia? Man, she's the cattiest girl in school."

"Yeah," John Jr. said. "She's pretty. I don't even mind if she has short hair, she is fine everywhere else."

"Yeah, everywhere," Willie replied, snatching the football away from John Jr. "Why don't you say hello and ask her out?"

"Are you kidding, she would never go out with me. Besides, she has a boyfriend."

"Yeah. She likes riding Ivy's fancy car," Willie said. "Yeah, you right. Girls like her don't go out with guys like us. Unless it's Blue—he gets anybody he wants."

"Blue," said John Jr. "Is he dating her?"

"No, John Jr., I mean, Blue will be going pro, and pro is money."

They watched the Corvette drive out of view. Savannah was jogging in their direction.

"Hey sis," Willie said. "What's wrong with you? You mad at Moe?"

"Moe," Savannah screamed. "Will you stop talking to me about Moe? I am looking for somebody."

"Who?" Willie asked.

"Don't worry about it," said Savannah. "I'll see you later at home."

"I'm going to John Jr.'s for dinner tonight." Willie said, smiling broadly. She waved at John Jr. "Oh, hello, John Jr.", she said, "I didn't see you." Her hips switched to the football field.

"Where is she going?" Willie said out loud, "John Jr. you are so lucky you don't have a sister. She is sad one day, happy another day, and every day she is a pain."

Laughter could be heard in cars driving by, friends walking by, John Jr. and Willie fleeting by to Chester Street.

Exodus for Blue was late and easy. He savored having the gym to himself, apart from Coach Elmore talking to a journalist. He cleared his locker, packed his gym bag. As good as naked, Savannah marched in. Her eyes were redder than her finger nail polish. "Blue, why didn't you speak to me," she hollered. "Don't you like me anymore?" Coach Elmore closed his office door. She sat on the flat bench, staring at his rock-hard legs.

"Savannah— that was last night; today, I don't want you, so stay away."

"What? You can't treat me this way. I don't understand." Blazing tears rolled down her coco-brown face.

All of a sudden, "Blue, son, what's going on?" Coach Elmore asked grimly.

"Nothing Coach," he returned harshly.

"Okay, well, I'll see you in January—Merry Christmas." With his briefcase and car keys dangling in his pants pocket, Coach Elmore left straightway.

"Savannah, I got to get out of here. Don't you have some place to go?"

She wiped her eyes with the palm of her hands. "I feel sick," she said.

Blue removed his jock underpants. "Maybe Moe can give you something to make you feel better; I told you it won't hurt the next time."

She bounced off the bench, her lungs reached the ceiling. "You pig." Teardrops smothered her face as she darted out the door.

Blue laughed. "See Megan, what you caused me to do? Every time you hurt me, I'm gonna hurt another." A white towel over his muscle toned shoulder, he rolled to the shower. In the warm water he sang, "All I want to be is to be with you, and baby I want you."

In the heat of the night, Big Boy Blue hit the brakes hard driving his Aunt Rose's '62 sky-blue Nova. He heard merriment in Megan's household. "Early still at seven o'clock," he said, "Aunt Rose has the lights out." He shuffled in the door. "I should go over to the Smiths and say hello. It's almost Christmas." Stomping to the Smith's front door, he heard Megan's voice and babbling from Willie. "Savannah's brother," he said, backtracking to his house.

Blue saw a note on the rosewood kitchen table. He shoved her cardboard hatbox full of Christmas cards to the side and sat on the table and read: "Blue, both hips are bothering me something awful so I wasn't able to cook dinner. I telephoned Mrs. Smith and asked her bring you supper. She promised she would. It's so humid, and I am tired. Don't forget to turn the kitchen light off. And make sure you leave the bathroom light on upstairs, your ninety-year old auntie forgets sometimes where she is."

He looked in the refrigerator, in the oven, and there was no plate set aside for him. "I supposed Willie is eating my dinner," said Blue scornfully. He turned the kitchen light out. The living room was dark; he opened the window for a soothing Southern breeze. His body slouched on the sofa, thinking of Megan's soft voice. "I'll take a fifteen minutes nap, and then go over and get my dinner," he mumbled. Embracing the Christmastime heat, he slept.

At the Smiths, dinnertime was jolly entertainment with Willie's jokes, in the middle of Creole pork chops, collard greens, cast-iron cornbread, and sharp cheddar macaroni on the sixty foot table. "Every time, I ask a girl out at school, she tells me I am too fat," Willie said, chuckling. "I got no money, and I don't even care. I say, I do have a smile and she says: Having a big smile don't help you none. My momma always tells me she likes my smile, and that does bring a girl around. What do you think Mrs. Smith?"

"Willie, your momma is right." Megan said, "A smile can get you more than money any day." She asked, "John Jr., what about you? Do you like girl in school?"

His eyes dared Willie. "No, there's nobody I like right now," John Jr. said.

Willie didn't scare, "John Jr. likes Sythia." Willie gulped his sweet lemonade. "But she got a boyfriend." John Jr. popped Willie on his forehead.

"That hurt." Willie reached for another piece of corn bread.

"Son," John said. "What's this girl Sythia look like?"

"She's real pretty and pleasing to look at, especially when she wears short skirts," Willie blurted out.

John Jr. smiled, staring at Megan. "John Jr., do you like this girl?"

"Mom, Willie is thickheaded; I never said I like Sythia. Besides, she has a boyfriend," John Jr. said quietly.

"Yeah, he's rich and drives a yellow convertible," Willie said grinning.

"Boys, perhaps, we should have a men-talk about girls," John said, and drew his arms around Megan.

"Girls," said Megan. "What do you know about girls?" She released her body from his clasp and went into the kitchen. Moments later, she returned with a coconut pineapple upside-down cake and laid it on the table.

Slicing the cake with her right hand, John held her left. He placed her hand on his chest. "The heart is where the girl is. Son, you get her heart, you got the girl," John said. Smiles were everywhere.

"John, really," Megan said, cutting a large piece of cake. Willie held his dessert plate. "Oh, I forgot to take Vinnie her dinner tonight. She's not feeling well. She sliced cake for husband and son. "John Jr., could you take over Mrs. Rose dinner for me," she asked, staring at his frowning face.

"Mom, she talks forever, and Willie is here." He looked at his father.

"Baby, I was just going to have a talk with the boys, and the basketball play-offs game is on tonight." John squeezed her hand.

"How could I forget about your basketball game," she sighed. "It's three against one." She unloosened her pale pink half apron. "I'll be right back," Megan said, "after the game." She watched John and John Jr. walking side by side to the family room. Willie collected the cake, and three bottles of Coca-Cola.

On her way to Mrs. Rose's house, she noticed the half-moon. Her black patent leather slippers got caught in the scrub and she almost fell. "Darn it," Megan said. Blue jumped immediately at the sound of her. She knocked on the door; he opened the door and pulled her in. "Blue," she said. His immense hands held her neck, kissing her. She was holding the dinner. "Blue Baby, I can't breathe, I am going to drop this plate." He seized the plate and placed it on the wooden African stool. He lifted her over his strong shoulders and her slippers fell to the floor. The old-fashioned sofa was cushy; her body oozed in.

"When is your husband leaving?" he asked. His hands touched her warm body.

"Blue, I don't know," she said, embracing his will.

"Look at what you are doing to me. When I see you, I got to have you," he said. "I can't help myself." They held one another, and before she realized it, he unzipped his blue jeans. All of him was inside of her. She did not complain, and she calmly came.

After some time together, they held hands as he walked her to the door. "Don't make love to him tonight," he whispered in her ear. She rested her head on his hard, steel chest. He ran his fingers through her radiant hair. "Good night," he said.

Before midnight, Big Boy Blue ate his dinner. Her smell was in the house, in his heart. Every mouthful was Megan. He remembered what his momma once told him, "Blue, a man got to have three things to make him happy: a good woman, good loving, and good cooking." Blue patted his hard stomach. "Momma, I got all three." He said, fiery.

At Midnight, Megan was lying in the bathtub blowing bubbles. John opened the door, holding a Corona beer. A white fragrance candle in a hurricane candleholder lay on the toilet seat. "Megan," he said. "How many times have I told you about the dangers of candles and closed doors?" She sat upright, stared above his close-shaven hair cut, and suddenly, the plush pink bathroom was silent. He gazed at her sensuous body. "Baby, can I come in?" He put down his beer on the wooden floor. Fighter pilot fingers fondled her wet fruity hair. He kissed her nude lips and she turned away. He removed his khaki shirt, showing maintained, muscled firmness. "Can I come in?" Tenderly, he asked.

"Baby, the water is cold now. Is the game over?" Megan asked, stepping out of the tub. John grabbed an Egyptian cotton towel, wrapped it around her body.

"John, I don't feel well," she said, lying on the fresh cotton sheets.

"What's wrong?" He asked soothingly.

"It's a secret. I can't tell you," she said coyly.

With that, he kissed her neck, her nipples.

"Stop John, my period is on," she said. "You know how you don't like the blood on the sheets."

He enraptured her navel. "I don't care this time," he said.

She tried not to like it, but she did. They delighted each other through the early dawn. Megan felt divine.

7

That morning, Megan thought, "Am I losing my mind: in love with two men?" Easing off the bed, she covered John's body with muslin blanket. She fastened her black velvet robe around her waist. "I'm going downstairs to start breakfast," she said. John awoke. "I bet you forgot Miss May Perry is coming over tonight for dinner," she said with a smile.

"I forgot," John said. "Baby, wake me after she is gone." John fixed the pillow on his face.

"John, she's the only family, I have—be nice," she anxiously said, and left the bedroom.

He mumbled, "What about your father?" He said to himself, "Let's not fight about her father this early."

Brewing dark Columbian coffee, Megan pondered, "Can I be in love with my husband and Blue? Miss May Perry will surely know if something is wrong. I got to get Blue out of my mind."

Like always, Big Boy Blue awoke to exercising: three hundred sit-ups, one hundred push-ups, weights, stretching. He dreamed of Megan, and the only remedy to waiting for her again was training hard. "Blue, your momma is on the telephone from Chicago," Mrs. Rose said. She creaked in, leaning on her walking cane. "She wants to wish you a Happy Christmas."

"What's so happy about Christmas? You don't even have a Christmas tree." he said, lifting a fifty-pound weight.

"Blue, a tree has nothing to do with Christmas. It's about the Savior, our Lord," she said.

"What lord, Auntie Rose? What you talking about?" He laughed.

"Blue, your momma wants to speak to you." She eased in her wicker rocking chair.

"Tell her I ain't home. I don't want to talk to her," he said, putting the weight down, grabbing an Eden Tigers jacket.

"Blue, she said you better talk to her, or she will fly to Georgia on Christmas day." He grabbed the phone.

"Yeah Mom," he said, irritated.

"Blue, what is that static on the line? Anyway, Baby, your momma misses you. I've been calling and worried about you."

"Worry about me, Mom, or worry about the football scholarships I been offered."

"Well, I heard something like that from some people, but that's not why I'm calling. I was wondering if you made up your mind where you're going to go next year."

"Why Momma?" he said.

"Well, I was told we could get more money from the Ohio State University, Baby."

"We, Mom?" he asked.

"I mean you Blue. I got a call from this agent, and he said if you sign with him, they would buy you a car, and could help me a little bit."

"Help you Mom," he asked. "I already helped you by leaving you with your man. Remember when you kicked me out and arranged for Auntie Rose to take me in?" Blue listened to her voice, tuned her words out and retraced his mind to Chicago.

"I was sixteen; I was a football superstar at Chicago High. Scholarship offers came from the top ten colleges in the United States. My mom left me alone and let me do what I wanted to. When I was in the eleventh grade, UCLA wanted me to enroll in their early admissions program; they offered her a generous incentive. Mom said yes. A week later, professional football teams countered the offer, and Mom gave in. She agreed I could play in Philadelphia. Principal Mitchell Wells protested, said I should finish my last year at Chicago High. "Besides," he said "your son is not eighteen years of age, Mrs. Bedford." My mom didn't like Principal Wells butting in, and said I was eighteen. She made an error on my official records. She showed Principal Wells my birth certificate, told him, there was nothing he could do about it. She stormed out of his office. But Principal Wells remained persistent, called me to his office. "Blue you are a powerful player. Why not graduate from high school, and attend college?"

Monday morning I was out of Chicago High, preparing for pro ball. That Thursday night, Mom said "Blue Baby, since you leaving anyway, my man Sweet Back is moving in." He came for dinner. The next hour, she howled. He opened her gate. She liked it rough, took the pain, he begged to rest—she howled the same.

On a cold Chicago morning, I smelled breakfast, hurried downstairs. Sweet Back was sitting back in my chair. He was eating steak, ham, eggs, home fries potatoes, and drinking Maxwell House coffee. Mom waved my plane ticket her hand. Sweet Back blew her a kiss. He gave me a slick grin, smiled. "Good luck," he said. I remember my dad's same smile before she kicked him out of the house, out of my life. "Mom," I said. "I changed my mind. I've decided to stay, finish my last year at Chicago High." She stared at Sweet Back. "I promised to deliver your ass, or else I don't get my money." I said, "Sorry Mom."

"Sweet Back," she screamed. "Give me some space." Sweet Back looked down at his plate, up at me, gripped his coat—strode out the door.

That night at nine o'clock, Mom telephoned Auntie Rose. "Blue is gonna come stay with you for a while." She booked me on the midnight train to Georgia. "Blue, you think you won." She paused. "I'll see you soon."

The sky was dark blue, white clouds breezing through. Mom stood at the door wearing a short white slip, long black wool stockings. She kissed me on the cheeks. Her breath smelled of garlic. "Blue, I'm sure gonna miss you," she said, smiling at Sweet Back slipping in. He popped ten knuckles. "Blue, make sure you stop by the Waffle House and get something to eat. I don't want my sister to think I don't feed my child." Mom stepped back, Sweet Back slammed the door.

He returned to her guileless voice: "Blue, I never kicked you out. I told you my sister is ninety-two-years old, living alone and she needed family nearby. Besides, I can't quit my job and move to Atlanta." She said jarringly. "That is until you make up your mind what you gonna do."

"Let me guess; your man is gone and left you this time." He said abruptly.

"Blue, Short Bobby Head" don't live here right now. I called to wish my son a Merry Christmas, and I thought I could find out how my baby is doing?"

"Yeah, Christmas is a few days away. I'm doing just fine." He grinned.

"Blue, I ain't doing fine, and if you don't make up your mind about where you going to college, I might be moving to Georgia."

"Look Momma, I'm eighteen years old, and I can decide where I am going. I don't need your approval."

"Is that right, you smart ass? Well, the university might think other-wise."

"Mom, as soon as I decide, I'll make sure you get some money."

"I was just checking on you, son. I got company over, but you have a nice Christmas, Baby. I'll call you again, and real soon."

Mrs. Rose had rocked herself asleep. Blue slammed the phone down. He dashed out the door. The baby-blue Nova speeded off in a split second.

That same moment, Megan peeked at Blue's wheels whirling from his house. A bitter chill ran throughout her body. "Blue, what's happening? What's wrong baby?" she asked silently. Attempting to block him elsewhere, she turned on the radio. She stood still, listening to Billie Holiday sing "Stormy Weather." "What a Blue holiday this is turning out to be," she murmured.

8

"She will arrive early; she always does," Megan said to herself as she opened the refrigerator, reached for the roasting pan. "Thank goodness, I sautéed the herbs in a plastic bag yesterday. She preset her oven at 350°F. She read her menu: leg of Lamb, wild rice, butternut squash and turnips with neck bones, shrimp bisque, fruit salad, buttermilk hush puppies, and black walnut pound cake. "I know I'm forgetting something, but what?" She opened the refrigerator, the freezer. "Vanilla ice cream," she exclaimed. "John will have to go to the grocery and get more; I can't bear them fighting over ice cream today."

Soft slippers stepped upstairs. John Jr. was asleep. John relaxed in the bed, reading the Atlanta Constitution.

"Baby, come sit next to me," he said.

"John, I have work to do; we have a guest coming for dinner. I have ironing, and you want me to sit and be pretty. I need you to go downstairs to make sure the home bar is stocked for this evening, and wake-up John Jr. I'm going in the shower," she said. "By the way, no breakfast this morning unless you make it," she smiled; he did not.

Newspaper disbursed about, he snatched his robe. He yelled through the half-opened door. "What is it with you and Miss May Perry? Whenever, she comes over, you get upset."

"John, please close the bathroom door and see if you can get John Jr. out of bed," she said. The water and Megan dribbled together. "I got to control myself," she whispered. "Blue Baby, please stay away, at least for today."

Sports section in hand, John strolled to his son's room. "John Jr., time to get up—your mother's request."

"But, Dad, it's Saturday," John Jr. said.

"You can't stay in bed. Your aunt, Miss May, is coming for dinner today. Your mom got lots of work to do and we have to help her. Besides, I'm making breakfast this morning," he said. "Let's go—I don't want your momma mad at me."

"Blueberry pancakes, Dad." John Jr. jumped off the bed.

"Yep," John said; "With lots of butter."

"Mom doesn't like too much butter, Dad."

"I know, but she's too busy to notice. Hurry, John Jr."

Megan was sitting in a white side chair, bare, towel-drying her hair. John entered their bedroom. He blinked, she barely smiled. He shut the door behind him, grasped the handrail. "Miss May Perry," John grumbled.

The remains of the morning she cleaned the rooms upstairs. Afterwards, she strode to her ironing room. She ironed John's shirts. Wearing the first one she pressed, she said, "I love his shirts. How it gives me comfort, security, I used to think." She stared at John's old Zenith radio clock; the time was ten o'clock. Her mind was someplace else; she detoured to the window to see if Blue's car was home. "No sight, no sound, that's good." She returned to the ironing-board steam. "I'll press a couple more shirts before trudging down-stairs. I always start with the collar." She resumed, "Spellbound, I was, when I saw John's sexy eyes, honey-brown skin, when I was eighteen. And not even his great-granddaddy's Greek and Aswan African nose or his baseball shoulders captured me. Rather, it was his lips—they enticed me, and there was no escape.

Portia, my best friend and I went to a ballroom dance at The Royal Peacock Club on a warm Saturday night on Sweet Auburn Street, September 19, 1953. It was my first time there, but Portia, who was twenty-two, had gone twice with her boyfriend. Somehow, she left me at the entrance, and I saw a tall handsome man in a soldier's uniform staring, smiling, and I did not smile back.

As a matter of fact, everyone in the elegant club was gazing at me. I wore a yellow satin halter dress, black, closed, high-heel shoes, white satin gloves, black clutch bag with a large crystal buckle envelope flap. I borrowed my mother's Victorian, pearl-encrusted hairclip, she trimmed my hair that morning and it was even at my waist.

Moments appeared to feel like hours, standing alone. John zeroed in on my sheer legs heading my way. The tumultuous phonograph played a track from the Count Basie Orchestra. "Hello, may I have this dance?" he asked.

I loved to dance, and my 5'7 heels happily leaped in his 6'2 handsome eyes. "Yes, thank you," I replied.

You're thanking me," he laughed. "I must be the luckiest guy in the world." The song I shall never forget was "Teach Me Tonight," because, that night, I fell in love.

We talked, we danced, and we ate together. I had to leave at ten o'clock. He asked for my address and told me he was visiting his parents, who had moved here from West Virginia. He explained he was a fighter pilot for the United States Air Force, temporarily stationed at Robins Air Force Base in Houston County, Georgia. I asked many questions, but the one I asked immediately was, "How long would you be in Georgia?"

I have to report on assignment in Europe in a few months," he said cheerfully.

I thought, "Perhaps, he doesn't like me." I was disappointed, and yet, relieved because there would be no way my father could worry about him.

The next day became every day John and I were together. The first week in December we wandered around Peachtree Park on a grey overcast Saturday. He kept his strong arms tight around my little-bitty waist.

"John, you are like me," I said. "I have no brothers or sisters, and we both like the blue sky, boundless trees, and the beauty of nature."

Right in front of the willow tree, he said, "Megan, you have everything I want in my woman—you are earthy and exquisite. I am in love with you. I never want to be another day without you." With a diamond ring in his hand, "Will you marry me?" he asked.

I had never kissed a boy, John was my first boyfriend. My momma, Lina, never once spoke to me about sex. I did know that she loved Daddy Windom, and I loved John.

My daddy was annoyed with me, because I did not attend college. He met his Lina—he used to say—at Savannah State University. They married after graduation in 1929 and moved to Atlanta. Her degree was in English literature, his degree, liberal arts. She became a homemaker, whereas he pursued a painting career.

He loved Edgar Degas' work; he believed he too had such talents. Eventually he became bitter and turned to bourbon. He hoped I would become a professional artist, and I practiced Mozart's piano concertos—four hours a day from the age of six to eighteen. John was even-tempered and calm when he met my daddy; I sensed he was not afraid of him. He demonstrated confidence; he was in control. Daddy Windom was intimated, and I found courage to leave home.

"Yes," I said. And on December 12, 1953, we were married. John had already closed on our house on Chester Street a month before he proposed. I married a twenty-eight-year-old man, college educated and an officer in the United States Air Force.

Living in Atlanta, I never saw ice storms, but on the morning in January 1955, we made love; the same moment I knew I was pregnant. John Jr. was born, Thursday, October 13, 1955.

As it is today, we have been married for twenty years. The handsomeness of his face has endured, and his mouth is mine. The only difference is his attractive, salt-and-pepper hair and reading glasses. In the early years of our marriage, we made love as if there would be no other day. It changed when he was away, and through the years he has been away. I think of it as having my husband for a brief vacation: It can be a week, months, or a long moment. I stopped expecting John to be home, and still, I hoped he would stay.

Deviating from her ironing, Megan strolled to the narrow bookcase with family photographs. She kissed Lina's picture. She still reminisced, "I wonder if I had gone to college, if that would have made my life any better." She poured water on John's shirt and started ironing the sleeves. "I think of my momma, I want to cry. Many times, I do, especially when John is on assignments. Daddy Windom stopped loving her and wanting her. My momma's spirit could not accept his lack of desire. She faded into a wonder world.

Lina taught me to start with the sleeves, and she was right. Gosh, when I was a young girl, I would sit down at the kitchen table and watch momma iron my daddy's shirts. If Miss May Perry came over, I sat and listened to them, while they drank black coffee with three teaspoons of sugar. Miss May Perry did most of the gossiping while momma ironed daddy's shirts. That's when momma was happy, and Miss May Perry was sad.

If there was mention of men, I was politely given an errand in the yard. Momma spent hours ironing Daddy's shirts. If there were one crinkle, Daddy, would throw it on the floor and grab another one. By the time I graduated from high school the summer of 1953, Daddy Windom was not around that much. Momma still ironed his shirts and kept burning them. Momma was sad all the time; Miss May Perry was happy. She met a thin dark-skinned man with straight black hair. He was rich and owned some land in Macon, Georgia. She didn't mind that his right hand was cut bad and you could see his bone. She got herself a man, he was seventy-three; she was fifty and soon to be married.

"He has twenty acres of land or about," Miss May Perry said. "Lina, child he's barely five feet and bony, but I don't care. He is a widower with no children." My momma smiled, and her sunny face started to look like shade. "Lina, what's wrong? You acting funny; I'm gonna take you to the doctor."

Momma burst out crying. "I don't know what's wrong; I keep forgetting how to iron Windom's shirts. He gets awfully mad at me, and sometimes don't come home."

"I'm taking you to the hospital and right now," Miss May Perry said. She drove us to the hospital; I sat in the back seat. We sat in the colored section at Grady Memorial Hospital.

"Mrs. Mutton will have to stay with us for tests until Saturday," the doctor said. That next Sunday, Miss May Perry and I had black coffee together.

"Megan, your momma is sick for sure. I am your godmomma; I will always be here for you." Momma never came back home, she stayed at the hospital until they moved her to Hampton Sanatorium. The week before, I had started dating John. Daddy Windom quickly moved his in with his girlfriend.

John and I visited with Momma every weekend, and even when he asked Lina if he could marry me. She seemed to know who I was, and what he said. The doctors didn't know what was wrong with Momma. Miss May Perry cried all the time; we cry together, because we both loved her so.

No matter what I am planning for the day, I make sure I iron John's shirts. I love the feel of fresh cotton shirts on my body; it brings back the romance we shared.

Sure, Miss May Perry is strong willed. "My momma became weak," she once said to me. "Lina loved your father, and did whatever to make him happy." I told her we were a family and happy once. She turned her head, and read *Ebony Magazine*.

Daddy Windom never visited momma in the sanatorium. Even before she passed away, he refused to see her.

Today, he doesn't look good. He is sixty-eight and looks eighty-eight. His woman never took care of him the way my momma did, and his shirts are never ironed; they don't even look clean.

I don't talk to Daddy Windom, but my husband does. He wants John Jr. to know his other grandfather. John reminds me that Windom never remarried, and feels he loved my momma. "That name makes me sick," I said.

Miss May Perry called a few years ago, and said she heard what my momma had is called Alzheimer's. I still don't understand the disease, but John keeps me updated. Miss May Perry is like my momma in ways that was the best of her. Except she don't need a man, like momma and me; she is rich, her husband is dead, and she is happy all the time.

I don't care what John says, I don't feel sorry for Daddy Windom, having cancer of the liver. He dropped my momma, and I dropped him.

The evening oozed with the sounds of Duke Ellington and John Coltrane's "In a Sentimental Mood." Megan was dressed in a black chiffon, ruffled dress. The music penetrated her body as she danced her smooth, shaved legs on the shiny hard, wooden floor. John Jr. watched his mom; John admired her moves.

"Dad, why does Mom always listen to jazz right before Miss May Perry comes over for dinner?" She stopped, switched her body to John; she extended her left hand to him; her right hand was on her hip. He pranced on over and held her waist as they danced together across the living room floor. They circled around and around until John Jr. yelled, "I hate this music."

Husband kissed wife's red-velvet lips, and she waved to her son. "John Jr., come dance with your folks." Megan laughed.

"Mom, I don't dance with my parents." He folded his arms and shook his head. They giggled, John swung Megan fast around him, holding her waist, she gazed at his eyes, and he carried her lips to his private whispers.

"Son, this is how I first got your mom to love me," John said.

"Dad, I thought you said Mom liked your uniform."

"Ha," Megan said. "His uniform! Is that what your father told you?" They danced loose, hands steady; Megan slowly moved closer. "Well, the uniform did help," she said. John kissed her cheeks.

She smelled the lamb, lunged to the kitchen. "Oh, thank God, it's fine." She yelled.

John came near, felt her behind. "Baby, it's the way I like it."

The doorbell rang. Excited, she said, "John Jr. turned off the record player, I'll get the door; John sweetheart, you stay right there." She paused for a brief second. "Miss May Perry," she vociferously said. Godmother hugged daughter.

"I hope I'm not very early," Miss May Perry said. "My driver was speeding, and I prayed until we were safe at the door. Megan, child, every time I see you, you look the same. I can't understand why you don't age and I do."

"Come on in Miss May, should we invite your driver in?"

"No child, he gets paid to sit and wait; that's his job. Where are your men? John Jr. is that you? Are you two inches taller than last summer? I don't believe it."

"I'm almost taller than Dad, Aunt May," he said. "I've been taller than Mom a long time."

John kissed Miss May Perry on her ruby cheeks. "Miss May, good looks run in Megan's family." John grinned.

"Good looks ain't got nothing to do with it; it's called Elizabeth Arden's night cream. I tell you though, John, you a handsome man. Shoot, it must be your wife's good cooking."

He kissed Megan's hand. "No Miss May, it's love," John said emphatically.

After dinner, they moved from the dining room to cocktails in the living room. Miss May Perry's clean French manicured hands held her bourbon.

"What time is it?" Miss May Perry said, while strolling to the front door.

"It is seven o'clock," John replied. "Are you worried about the traffic?"

"Honey-child, traffic is not my concern. I want to make sure my driver is not falling asleep. I'm paying him good money." She opened the door, stood in the doorway, and in her high pitched voice said, "Lord have mercy, who is that young thing talking to my driver?"

In a split second, John stepped next to her. He waved to Blue. "He is our neighbor's nephew." Megan resembled a mannequin; she sat colder than her white marble coffee table. She managed to pour herself a full glass of white, Bourgogne Chardonnay.

"Dad," John Jr. screamed from his room. "What about the movie, 'Blacula?' I told Willie we would meet him at Greenbriar Mall. He's eating at Chick-fil A restaurant."

"Let's go, I'm ready." John said. "Ladies, I'm sure you won't miss us." John Jr. raced to the bottom of the stairs, his Eden Tiger jacket in his hand.

"See you later Mom and Aunt May." He hopped out the door. "Hey, Dad," John Jr. hollered.

"Baby, let's hope the movie is sold out." He blew a kiss to Megan. "Miss May, be careful on the road, call us when you are home," John said.

"Dad, hurry, we're going to miss the movie," John shut the door.

A hidden silence set in between them. Miss May Perry sipped her bourbon, stirred the ice. The next moment, she laid her drink on the table. "Child, what is going on?" she asked.

"How is your blood pressure? Are you better?" Megan said, and accidently grabbed her godmother's glass. She gently placed it down; reached for her wine.

"Megan, let me tell you, if I lived next door to a body like that, my blood pressure would be mild to moderate and stay high. I am seventy-two-years old and I don't care about men, but if I thought...well, never mind. I now understand why lately you have been too busy to talk to me on the phone. You have been avoiding me. What's his name child?"

"Big Boy Blue," she whispered.

"And are you letting him be with you?

"I try not to let him in," Megan said. "I find myself wanting him, and so I give in."

"Child, are you crazy? You must promise me to end this affair tonight." She leaned forward, clinched Megan's hangs.

"John is a good-looking man, a good provider, and a damn good father and husband. You better forget about that big boy."

"Miss May, what am I going to do? Even now, I feel him."

"Megan, how old is he?"

"He's eighteen," she said, starring at the Christmas tree.

"That's one year older than your son." Miss May Perry screeched. "If your husband found out, and your son found out, you would be out that door."

She rested her head on Miss May Perry's stern shoulder. "Megan, is he worth you losing your family? Child, you are something else." Miss May Perry kissed Megan's forehead. "Enough foolishness, I'm going home. I will be alone in my godforsaken property, a house keeper I don't like, and a driver who's trying to kill me. But I am no fool. For if I was, I would be like you— wishing for the wonders of wonderland."

They hugged; Megan wiped her tears. "You're right; it's over."

"Good, I'm tired. I love you, and I love your family." She squeezed Megan's wedding-band hand. "Honey-child, you got to let him go."

By twilight, Megan still could not sleep. She woke her husband and showed him how much she loved him. By sunlight, she felt she heard Big Boy Blue's voice. She turned over, and her husband hungered more. She got on top of John and road him long until the lust of Blue was gone.

Christmas Eve morning was the smell of simple pleasures at the Smiths' house. Megan, baking banana bread; John, decorating with the Christmas lights in the front yard; John Jr., wrapping his parents' gifts, swallowing extra-sweet ice-tea in his bedroom.

It was ten o' clock, Megan stood in the front doorway. "John Baby, the telephone is for you."

"Okay, I'll be there in a minute," he said, while adjusting an illuminated whimsical Santa on the front porch. He opened the screen door. "Baby, I'll take the call upstairs."

"Hello," John said.

"Merry Christmas, Captain Smith. This is Second Lieutenant Hamilton. I was commanded to call you on behalf of Colonel Saddleback."

Pulling out the calendar in his desk, John peered at the red circle, February 1, 1973 back to work. "No problem, Lieutenant, Merry Christmas to you and your family."

With a knock at the door, Megan entered. "Baby, I brought your coffee. When you finish, come down for breakfast."

"Thanks Baby," he said. She left and returned to kitchen.

"Hold a moment, Lieutenant," John closed the door.

"Go ahead, Lieutenant," John sat at his desk, sipping his coffee."

"Sir, the colonel has instructed me to tell you, he needs you to report to duty tomorrow at Dobbins Air Reserve Base, exactly at 17:00 for a special assignment. Details will be explained by the colonel, sir. He also wanted me to wish your family a Merry Christmas."

"I understand Lieutenant. Please inform the colonel, I will be there."

"Yes, sir, thank you, sir." John hung up the phone. He relaxed his legs, finished his coffee. "If there is a God, please pray for me, that my wife does not get mad," he said silently to himself.

Another knock on the door, "Dad, Mom is calling for us, I'll race you downstairs."

"Yeah, in your dreams," John said.

Louis Armstrong and Bing Crosby singing "White Christmas" on the radio, Megan was humming alone, as well as hopping grits, bacon, scrambled cheese eggs, and sweet potato biscuits. She poured fresh squeezed orange juice in three crystal glasses.

"Mom, no pancakes?" John Jr. asked, reaching for biscuits.

"John, Jr., you cannot eat pancakes for breakfast every day." Megan stared at John who walked in the living room, turning on the Christmas tree lights. "Baby, it's early for the lights to be turned on."

"It's the best tree we ever had, Megan."

"John, you are always fussing about the light bill, and now you don't care."

"Today is special, and besides, I only fuss about the light bill eleven months out of the year."

"Come and eat your breakfast before it gets cold."

"Yeah, Dad, before, I eat your bacon," John Jr. said, grinning.

She studied John's face throughout breakfast. "I want to be a good wife and good mother to my son," she thought. "Thank you, Miss May Perry."

"Mom, I'm finished," John Jr. exclaimed. "Willie, some guys on the team are meeting at "College Park Mall" later."

"John Jr., it's Christmas Eve, why not hang around with your folks?"

"Mom, we plan to see a different movie every day, at a different mall, until we go back to school."

"What? That's ridiculous, son," she said. "And very expensive; right John?"

"It's okay," John said. He pulled out a twenty-dollar bill and handed it to John Jr. "I was going to give him few extra dollars for his Christmas present."

"Man, you the best, Dad. I'm gonna get ready and call to check on my ride. John Jr. grabbed two slices of bacon and ran swiftly upstairs.

"John, how much money are you going to give our son for Christmas?"

"Does it matter, Baby? He's happy and I'm proud of him."

She gathered the dirty dishes, put everything in the sink, and cleaned the table. There was silence. "Baby, I got a better Christmas present for you, but you got to wait for it tonight." She turned to face him.

"John, I don't need Christmas presents, I'm just happy you're home," she said. She rubbed his scrubby face. He drew her to him. She rested her head on his chest.

"I love the sound of your voice, the smell of your Chanel perfume; I can see your smile millions of miles away." John said. He stared at the kitchen table.

"Your wealthy son is upstairs, remember," Megan giggled.

"He's leaving soon. Why else would I arrange to get rid of him?" John kissed her ears, her neck. He pinned her body against the counter.

Stomping feet were heard galloping down. "Mom what time is dinner?"

She slipped away from John; he held onto her hand. "John Jr., could you be home no later than six o'clock? It's family-only tonight." Their hands hung as one. Their son hurried out. They stood in the doorway and waved good-bye. John closed the door and they strolled to the kitchen.

"Megan, our son is handsome, smart; he gets everything good from you." He held her behind, she unbuttoned his starched shirt.

"My chest is waiting for you." Megan kissed his hard nipples. John unloosened her lavender Jersey knit robe. Her floor-length white satin slip was split to the knees. His hands massaged her inner thighs.

"Baby let's go upstairs," Megan said.

"I can't wait that long," and he laid himself on the solid birch table.

In her mind, she thought, "He is strong, the same man." They both had a new kind of hunger for one another. "John, stay with me," she said. He carried her to their bedroom. "John," she said again.

"Baby, I'm here. You are my lady," he replied ardently. They loved each other from morning to mid-afternoon.

9

As soon as he awoke, grey skies were the start of his Christmas morning. John had been awake since four o' clock working, wondering how bad his day would end. This was not the Christmas present he hoped for. Nevertheless, he prepared to leave his family Christmas afternoon. He packed his suite case; he looked at his wife sleeping.

Minutes passed fast, he carried his one piece luggage downstairs and secured it in the closet. His uniform was already pressed behind his dark gray wool coat. Megan always made sure his black leather shoes were shined; side-by-side stood his black umbrella he brought back from Korea in 1953. It was his lucky umbrella; it reminds him of a life he loves.

He set his military watch for 15:00, and at that time, he would tell his family he has to report to duty today.

Turning his feet to the kitchen, he tapped his right knuckles on the farmhouse table where they made love yesterday. "I want her every day. There may never be another," he said. "I remember being mesmerized by her moves. I'd traveled around the world and had never seen legs like Megan's. She is sensual in every way I want her to be." While brewing Guatemala Antigua coffee, he returned back to his worries. "The Lieutenant did not give me any clues where I was going, or how long this journey would be. I know it's time I let these adventures go. I have two loves, my family and the Air Force. Megan is still a young woman of thirty-seven, and if she ever left me…" He paused. "What am I doing, doubting her love, doubting myself, before I get out the door? I always, do this to myself, 'Soldier's Stew,' I call it. He pulled out two porcelain cups, placed them on a silver tray. "Don't forget, sugar, she likes it sweet."

He entered their bedroom and stared at her lusty body holding two pillows. The other two queen pillows lay on top of the Oriental rug; silk stockings he bought for her were on top of a rectangular red box. "She couldn't resist and took a peak at her present," he smiled. Vigorous legs crossed in his leather chair, drinking coffee, enjoying her luster. She awoke at third sip. "I thought, I was dreaming and found myself drowning in the smell of your coffee." He carried her cup over to her, sat close.

"Baby did you put sugar in it?" she asked.

"Taste it," he replied.

"Mmm, I love the way you make coffee. When you are not home, I miss it the most."

His captain's hands touched her chin. "I love watching you rise in the morning, and when I am away, I miss you the most."

She kissed his fingers. "Sweetheart," she said, "Merry Christmas."

"Do you like your silk stockings, Baby?" Rubbing her thighs, he held one pair.

"You know I do, John," she said. He slid the stockings on her legs as she slowly drank her coffee.

"Can I give you your special present now?"

"Baby, after dinner—let's exchange presents then."

"This, I would like to see you wear, the way you look this moment." He walked to his black briefcase, unlocked it, and handed her a gold box. "It smells of sweet perfume." She leaned against his broad shoulders, unwrapped the purple linen napkin. "John," she hollered.

"I saw it when we landed in Geneva; it was moonlight and I thought of you." In the palms of her hands, Megan smiled at the key pendant with diamonds. She lifted her hair. "John, do you like it with my hair up or down."

He touched her nude lips. "I like it anyway you wear it."

"John, I love you," Megan said. She guided his keen hands to her key. He climaxed, his heart palpitated fast. She wiped his forehead. "Baby calm down," she said. "We have all day, it's Christmas." John closed his eyes.

At noon time, the Atlanta's WAOK radio station played Nat King Cole's "The Christmas Song." With the volume high, Megan prepared dinner, pausing temporarily to stroke her diamond necklace. The music stopped abruptly: "This is an important weather announcement, the entire metropolitan area, College Park area, DeKalb County, and throughout Georgia is expecting a major thunderstorm by two o'clock. Be careful out there driving, folks, on Christmas Day. Stay tuned for further announcements—now back to the holiday program." Megan switched the music off. "This day, I'm too happy to worry about the weather," she said. "How is my honey-baked ham?" She opened the oven. "Perfect, I must say—it's heavenly."

The day progressed; John Jr. strolled in the kitchen showing off a new navy wool coat.

"Mom, this coat is gonna be too hot for Georgia. It never gets cold enough for a heavy wool coat, but I like it."

"I told your father the same thing. He wants his son to have a coat similar to his."

He turned his collar up. "I might wear it to the Christmas party later."

"John Jr., the weather is going to be bad out there tonight. I don't want you driving in the rain on Christmas."

"Mom, we will be inside, not outside."

"That's fine John Jr., however, ask your Dad if it's okay."

"I did already. He said I could go out."

She removed her red organdy apron. "He did?"

"Dad said we would be having dinner at three o'clock and I could leave right after to meet my friends."

She reached for her scissors, cut off the tag on his coat. "He did," she said quietly. Stomping boots could be heard from the staircase.

John Jr. met his dad's eyes. "Dad, can I still go to the party after dinner?"

"Yes, John Jr. The coat fits you well."

"Thanks, Dad." He bumped John on his way to the family room. The television could be heard in the kitchen.

Her muted lips moved passed John to the wood countertop. She opened two cans of creamy dark chocolate frosting. "Are we having chocolate cake for dessert, Baby? Everything smells good in here. How much longer for dinner?"

She poured milk and broke two eggs in a yellow ceramic bowl. Suddenly her hands froze. John's elbows leaned on the stained table: he kept an eye on her.

"Are you leaving today?" She sat in the side chair.

"I was going to tell you later—I received an order. I have to leave this afternoon, Baby."

She leaped from the wooden chair; her hands grasp the top of kitchen counter. Tears fell on her cheekbones; immediately, she opened the oven door, sprinkled brown sugar on the ham. "What time do you leave?" She shut the oven door.

"Baby, don't cry. I feel awful. I have no choice, and I got to obey orders."

They could hear John Wayne's voice on the television, John Jr. yelling to the tube. "I'm due to report to the base at five o'clock." John said. "I figured we could have dinner by three o'clock. That would give you and me some quiet time to be together."

Her pink nails caressed her diamond necklace. "We had our quiet time this morning. Now, you are telling me, we only have a couple hours on Christmas Day to be a family."

Water flowed down her swollen eyes. Thunder and lightning burst through the sky. The electricity was out throughout the house.

"Hey, Dad, it's crazy out there. Mom, I hope the telephone works. I'm gonna call Willie to see if there's still a party." He skipped to his room. Darkness seeped in their house, in John's heart, in Megan's mind.

"John, why don't you call and see if you have to come in. The weather is awful—how can you fly in this storm?"

He delicately kissed her nails. "Baby, I love you. That's why I have to go to work. It's how I take care of my family. I can't call in—I'm an officer. Weather is never an obstacle; I have flown in blizzards, bombs flying over my head, and bodies falling on me. How could I disobey an order, my responsibility, and my honor?"

"You are a solider first, a father second, and a husband last." She wrapped her arms around her chest. He embraced his arms around her waist. He kissed her. She turned her head away. His hand brought her lips to his. She kissed his neck, he unbuttoned her blouse, unsnapped her bra. His left hand made room for himself underneath her billowy skirt, and his right hand unzipped his pants. Her back firm against the floral wallpaper, and he pressed and pressed.

"John, you are hurting me." She pushed her palms against his chest.

He stopped. "You don't want me anymore?" He stared in her eyes and quickly stepped aside.

She buttoned her blouse, exited the kitchen. He flattened his head on the wall. Wails of fear twisted his stomach.

And yet, he followed her to their bedroom. She locked the bathroom door. He heard her tears. "Baby, open the door. I'm sorry I have to leave on Christmas." The house returned bright, street lights remained black. "Baby," he said. He waited. He heard the steady sound of water. "I'm in my own war room." Thinking out loud, his shoes stepped out.

A brisk knock on the door, "You okay, son?"

"Dad, be for real, every time there is a storm, the lights blink out in Georgia. Besides, Willie said the party is still going on. Can I go? I told Willie you leave today, and Mom doesn't want me to drive. So, his mom is picking me up."

"That's fine, son."

"Dad, what's wrong? You looked tired."

"Nothing is wrong? I'm going to take a nap. Make sure you come and say goodbye to your parents before you head out."

Lying on their white linen bed, John raised his head to the ceiling counting the railing that could be heard from Megan.

He stopped thinking and fell asleep. He heard a knock at the door and leaped to the bathroom. It was locked.

"Dad, Mom, Willie's outside." John Jr. said. We're leaving."

John was dressed in a green wool Air Force uniform. "Give me a hug son."

"Dad, you look great. I can't wait to wear my uniform. Where's Mom?" The car horn blew. "Dad, I got to go. Oh yeah, will you tell Mom I'll be back by curfew at ten o'clock."

They hugged, and John's eyes were building bits of water. "Dad, will you be home for New Years?"

"I hope so son. I'll call and let your Mom know as soon as I know."

The car horn blew again. "Merry Christmas, Dad. Thanks for my big wallet for Christmas."

"Tell Mrs. Penn, I said to drive carefully."

"We're used to this weather—but I'll tell her. See you later."

He knocked on the bathroom door. "Baby, please open the door, and let me say good-bye." He waited. "John Jr. promised to be home at ten o'clock." It was three o'clock. He didn't wait. He walked down the staircase, buttoned his wool coat, and grabbed his hat. The Christmas tree lights blinked in harmony: orange, white, and gold. He touched an angel dangling on the Noble fir tree. It fell; he bent down and saw his name on a gift from Megan. He looked at the wooden stairs, candy cane stockings hung on the handrails with John Jr., Mcgan, and his name. He took off his hat and coat, dashed to their bedroom.

"Megan, I'll call you when I know where I am. I love you, and you are first, never last, in my heart." She unlatched the door. Her long waves were wantonly on her shoulders. He stared at the gray silk-chiffon slip which drooped at her feet. With each step, he sniffed *Joy* perfume. "The last drop," he thought, "I bought for her in Paris eleven months ago."

She wrapped her arms around his waist. "I love you, John," she said fervently. Her warm welcoming body tempted him to stay. She kissed him deeply, desperately. He was in danger. Hurriedly, he unfastened her arms.

"Baby, I love you," John said rapidly. "I'll call you from Dobbins Base." And he was out the door.

The wind was blowing, barking on Chester Street. Megan heard John's Mustang Pony cranking and then no more. She bundled up in her velvety robe, hands sliding down the handrail skipping over the Christmas stockings. The house was scented with honey baked ham and chocolate cake. She set the dining table for one. She stared at the centerpiece of yellow roses, the silver candelabrum, and drank three glasses of Nicolas Feuillatte Champagne.

And after dinner, she turned the house lights out except for the Christmas lights. She strolled into the living room with the champagne bottle in her hand. Her robe hung off her shoulders, sweeping the floor. "I can't take this rain," she screamed, and placed her finger in her ear. She glared at the record player. "Charles Brown, I need to hear you." The song stirred her body; she sang the lyrics aloud, "Merry Christmas Baby, You Sure Look Good To Me."

The rolling sounds of thunder, lighting stormed at the door, blackout on the street, soaring music, she walked barefoot to the kitchen. She sliced the largest piece of chocolate cake she could hold in her hands and trailed to the living room. Sitting on the sofa, she opened her present from John Jr., smiling at the book titled, "*All Color Books of Birds*." Startled, the Christmas tree lights popped, the record player stopped.

There was a harsh thump at the door. "John, he's come back." She rushed. He was drenched and she desired him. His wet hand wiped the chocolate crumbs clean off her mouth, and he kissed her at the door.

Her body boldly ascended to the stairs. "Big Boy Blue," she said. "Bring the champagne bottle with you, and Baby, leave everything else at the door."

In the murky house, Megan turned over to John's side and saw Blue. She panicked and pranced to the shower. Several minutes lapsed; she snuggled in John's terry cloth bathrobe, and tip-toed into her son's bedroom. He was still out with Willie; it was nine-thirty. She tramped over to her bed. "Blue, you got to get up and leave. John Jr. will be home in a few minutes." Blue rolled over and did not answer. "Blue, please, my son will be home soon."

"Your husband left you, you wanted me, and I am here." His eyes were sparking like a sharp stone. "Come here."

"Blue, I want you to leave."

His athletic shoulders were direct; his knees bent, and his stardust eyes scanned the room. Three other moments they had made love in Megan's bedroom, this moment it's their bedroom—the Queen-sized bed, framed panels on the side boards, and foot board stained in dark brown; the mahogany wood desk, a silver frame wedding picture of Megan and John, alongside a family photograph with John Jr. holding a football, and medals framed on the wall; the grey stone fireplace had a black-and-white sketch of Megan framed in gold leaf. And white chiffon curtains dangling from the wide ten-foot windowsill to the blue and brown rug on the hardwood floor.

He turned to her and caught her eyes immersed in his massive muscular body. Blue sensed his power. Her hair was wet, and she smelled new. He observed that the rust robe overwhelmed her.

She looked at the clock radio; the time was nine forty-five. "Blue, John Jr. will be here in fifteen minutes, please dress and leave."

He laid his chocolate face on her mint-green pillow and remembered when his Aunt Rose was a librarian at Ralph Bunche Middle School. He was eight years old and every Sunday she telephoned him in Chicago to talk about people he didn't care about. She started with W.E.B. Du Bois, Fredrick Douglas, and Dunbar. It worked for two months, until Aunt Rose stopped sending Mom money after her husband died. Mom said "Blue is gonna be rich playing football, what the hell he need history for anyway?"

Time after time, he ignored his Aunt Rose. Today her words inspired his iron will. "What time will he be home?"

"Soon, Blue, soon." He pulled the sash around her waist and threw her body on the bed. "Tell me how bad you want me to go."

Bell chimes were ringing in her head. Megan's mind was no longer hers. They loved each other like lovers in love. He dressed, gazed at her abundant beauty, and desired more time. Blue's moist lips kissed Megan's baby lips.

"Don't treat me like a child; I am a man," he said securely.

She heard a car. "Blue be a man and leave." He would not jeopardize having her again; he ran down the stairs, and she behind him.

His hands grasped the basement knob and hers the front and they opened their doors.

PART II

10

John drove too fast from Atlanta on the black highway through some burned-out trees and scattered, dimmed lights. The sky was dark, dancing with the rain and his racing heart. He could not concentrate on the road because Megan was on his mind. His brain and body were straining, and for the first time he thought, "I'm endangering my edge as a pilot when my soul is worrying about her. I'm going to have to keep my word and retire next year." When he arrived at Dobbins Air Force base in Marietta, Georgia, Second Lieutenant Hamilton was waiting and talking to Colonel Saddleback in his office.

Colonel Saddleback sat behind his grey metal desk on a black, high chair, smoking a Cuban cigar. Second Lieutenant Hamilton stood erect, blowing smoke away from his twenty-two-year old face. John knocked on the door, saluted Colonel Saddleback. "Good evening Colonel Saddleback, Captain John Smith reporting for duty, sir."

"I hope my cigar smoking don't bother you like this young start-up, Captain. When it rains like the monsoon, my mind is back to 1947 Japan, and my body is directing bombs to our enemy. These expensive Cuban cigars are the only thing that relaxes me in this thunderous rain." Second Lieutenant Hamilton didn't blow anymore smoke from his face; he coughed.

"This is what we fought for," Colonel Saddleback said. "So, young 'Butter Bars' can cough their way on the reserve. Now, Captain Smith, I regret having to bring you in on Christmas Day." Colonel Saddleback placed his cigar down and turned his back from them and stared at the rain. "Captain, we got a problem, and tonight it's your problem. Tell me, how was your family? My family gave up on Christmas and me years ago."

"My family is fine, and thank you for asking sir."

"I remember those days disappointing my wife, and I haven't seen a Christmas tree in our home in twenty-five years. Well, Captain, your problem is this damn rain and having to take off in the F-4 Phantom II in an hour. Then you got to drop cargo off in England, later in West Germany, and wait and pick up cargo in Italy. We are talking about classified supplies and from there you will bring the cargo back to the United States. Since you have flown many high level assignments in Korea, I know you will handle everything with great care. This is our lieutenant's first classified trip, and if he can't stand to be in a room with smoke, how the hell can he fly on a day like today? And, knowing the urgency and emergency of the situation, I had to call you in on Christmas Day."

The colonel turned around and resumed smoking his cigar. "Lieutenant, go out there, bring two black coffees, while I explain in detail to the captain, his mission." At ease, Captain, and sit down. Lieutenant, hurry; we need our coffee." John watched Hamilton run out and remembered when he, too, was young 'Butter Bar.' Colonel Saddleback laughed. "In twenty years he will be tormenting another young lieutenant." He ceased smoking and placed his cigar in a Japanese jade tray. "Captain Smith, the mission manifest is XLE, XWG, and XLI." He opened his desk drawer with a three-quarter inch-cooper key, and he handed two 3x2 stainless steel canisters to John. "Open the canister, Captain Smith." John's eyes lit like a Christmas tree. "You have four trigger weapons in each canister that are to be transported to Europe. In your hands are the XLE to be dropped off in England and the XWG in West Germany. In Italy, your contact will deliver to you the XLI, and you will return the canister back to me. Your secret cargo is for your eyes only, and again, let me repeat, Second Lieutenant Hamilton is unaware of the real cargo. Lieutenant Colonel Rossini will meet you at the Rome Ciampino Airport Base. He is stationed at Aviano Air Base; however, I requested him to meet you in Rome. Of course, we do not use our Phantom supersonic jet for regular cargo, but we do need a skilled and fearless fighter pilot for this mission. I will speak to you directly if there is a change in transporting your cargo. I am mighty glad you joined the Air Force Reserve several years back, the Reserve is the wing man for the Air Force."

"Colonel, sir," Hamilton said. "The coffee machine is not working, but there is tea, sir."

"Tea? That's punishment. See what I mean Captain? We would never allow a machine to prevent us from our coffee."

"Yes sir," John said. He grasped his cargo.

In twenty-two years of flying, John could have used an experienced co-pilot as his partner tonight, and it had nothing to do with the monsoon. "I want to be with my wife, making love and not war for the Air Force," he said in his mind. And still, he sat in his icy cockpit, helmet fastened. "No time for the past, this is now, Baby." he said out loud. "Hamilton, watch, beware, don't see the rain. See your friend, your father, and if you don't have either, let it be fear that keeps you alive."

Captain Smith skirted off in the F-4 Phantom II jet. He was confident, in control of the sky. "Nothing is going to get in my way, not even Christmas Day," he said vociferously.

11

Rome, Italy on New Year's Eve was nippy when John and Hamilton landed at the Rome Ciampino Airport at six-thirty in the morning. They had been flying for three days throughout Europe, dropping off their cargo. The Lieutenant Colonel, Roberto Rossini met them two minutes after they jumped out of their seats.

"Captain Smith, good morning. I have Colonel Saddleback on the phone in my office. Follow me please." John and Hamilton carried their glistening white helmets in one hand and brown leather United States Air Force jackets in the other. John smelled the sensational Italian coffee flowing through his veins.

"Colonel, do you think I may have some coffee?"

"Ah, yes, as soon as you speak to your colonel, please step into my office."

Second Lieutenant Hamilton proceeded. "No, only Captain Smith, please wait a second and have a seat." Hamilton stood outside the door, and John picked up the telephone.

"Captain John Smith here, Colonel, sir."

"Captain Smith, Rossini informed me, your cargo is not ready for departure today. He cannot confirm if you will have it in your hands by tonight or tomorrow. This is regrettable; however, I can trust that you will cooperate with Colonel Rossini." He coughed, "That's all, captain." The line cut off.

"Sir, may I use your telephone to call the United States," John asked.

"Of course, I'll have my assistant connect the call for you. Please write down the number."

In less than a minute, Vittorio entered the office. "Captain Smith, your call is ready. He sat in Rossini's Roman 19th-century chair.

He touched his beard and thought of her breast. "Hey Baby."

"John, where are you? Are you coming home for New Years?"

"No, I'm stuck in Italy, and I don't know if I'll be home tomorrow or in a few days.

"Oh," she said.

"I know, Megan. This was not my plan for New Years either. I promise it won't be next year."

"John you say the same words year after year."

"Baby, I'll make it up to you, but I can't talk long. I wanted to say, Happy New Year, and please give our son a hug for me."

"Okay, John."

"Megan, I wanted to say, I miss you more than you'll ever know, and I love you."

She took a moment. "John, Happy New Year." A quick click, she saw John Jr.'s bent-over body attempt to walk in her bedroom.

"Mom, I don't feel well," he said. She ran to him, he fell in her arms. Driving without stopping for red lights, she drove her white Mustang to Crawford W. Long Hospital.

In Rome, Hamilton stood rock-still waiting for John. Minutes later, he waved to Hamilton to come in the colonel's office.

"Yes Sir." He saluted.

"Hamilton, let's go to our hotel, shower, and meet up later for some real coffee."

"Coffee sir, I don't like coffee."

"Believe me, when you parachute over 100 hours flying, you will learn to love coffee like the finest legs you have ever seen. And, we are in Italy; they have the best coffee in the world."

"I rather have some fine legs, sir."

"Yeah" and they laughed exiting Rossini's office.

The cathedral ceilings in Hotel Cesare's lobby blended Greece and Rome—ancient Mediterranean architecture. The small, quaint hotel was a favorite of John's from his first visit ten years ago. He sometimes fell asleep on the red velvet Roman sofa, and the hotel manager tapped him on the shoulder to remind him he had a room. Flying all day and fearing he may not live another, exhausted upon landing, he could not move until the manager tapped him harder the next time. It was fifteen miles away from the base, and not too far away for any emergencies. "Most guys did not like it. They complained it was too small and not enough women walked by." John thought, "But for me, it's the quiet streets, antique shops, and coffee specialties that gives me peace, reminds me of home." If he was not resting, he walked the cobblestone streets watching lovers drinking and dancing to their dreams. "How often I promised Megan I would bring her here; we would explore the Arch of Titus, the Temple of Saturn, and the Temple of Romulus together." She would say, "John Jr. needs me at home." "True," he said. "I want her home to take care of our son."

He paused, stared at his watch. "Today is New Year's Eve, I miss the sweetness of her skin—her luscious legs. It's becoming harder to stay away from her." He removed his shirt and pants, place them neatly in a reproduced da Vinci-painted chair. The single brass bed was aesthetic, yet small for his frame. The mushy mattress sunk his back deep; he grabbed the wool olive-green blanket, and bundled on the floor. "I'll take a quick nap." He twisted, turned, and closed his eyes. "This feels like the wooden floor in my tent." He turned on his right side and whispered, "Even then, this was the only way I could sleep in Korea."

Several moments passed by, his eyes were shut. "I was flat down on the cold cot, cuddled in my sleeping bag at 0200 in late November 1950. I couldn't sleep because my heart was beating faster than my mind. I kept hearing my stomach growl as if voices were inside of my chest having a conversation about me. I had an hour before my early morning mission brief with Senior Commander, J.V. Pitts about pursuing MiG pilots over the Yalu River between the North Korea-China borders.

I kept thinking about the two pilots who ventured in the same direction yesterday, and they did not return to Kimpo Airfield. The leader and his wing man were shot down, setting the gas tank on fire, and spurted straightaway into the snowy blue waters. Two MiG Chinese fighter pilots scored their aerial "kills" and returned to their base without damage.

Bobby Jack and Tex Rod had been at Kimpo since bombing ranges off the West Coast of Korea in 1948. Their bond was tighter than a marriage band, and Commander Pitts often spoke about their potent strength to survive and stay alive. I wondered what words the Commander would say that Friday morning two years later to his 455th Fighter Squadron.

My roommate, wingman, and best friend, Handsome Joe, slept like a baby. He is from New York; he was used to living in the cold and adjusted to any kind of weather.

I glanced at my watch and turned my head on the raw pillow. "Why did I sign up for the Civilian Pilot Training Program at West Virginia State, anyway? Oh, yeah, in my freshman year at school Elia Martinez signed up, and he talked me into joining.

W. D. Moore

My father, James Duke, worked at a synthetic rubber company in Charleston, West Virginia, and Sundays were his only days off. After breakfast, he lied down with his weekly *Chicago Defender* reading out loud; one particular story regarded a Negro pilot, Eugene Jacques Bullard. My dad held his double whisky in his hand.

"Bullard joined the French Air Force in 1917, shot down a German aircraft, offered his services to the U.S Army, and they turned him down."

"Dad, why didn't you try to join the Air Force?"

He and his whisky walked over to me. "You see these glasses I been wearing them all my life? I was born with glasses. But you, nothing is wrong with your sight. You got perfect eyes—why don't you try?"

I was not sure if he was trying to encourage me or evict me from our house. In 1944, I was attending my freshman year at West Virginia State for Negroes, and planned to look for a job. He said, "As soon as you graduate, you got to leave my house. Don't look at your mother for help; my father pushed me out right after high school. I ain't feeding you once you get that degree."

When the government-sponsored Civilian Pilot Training Program (CPTP) ruled that six Negro colleges could be included, West Virginia State for Negros was one. I enrolled in March 1944, and the requirement was to enroll in advance private flight training, and sign an agreement to enter military service after graduation from college.

I graduated from college in June of 1948, and found a job at Kanawha Airport in Charleston cleaning commercial aircrafts. On the weekends, I hung around the airport observing the pilots, planes, and planning my future to become an aviator.

Six months later, I was ordered to Mather Air Force Pilot Training in Sacramento, California.

My last morning living at home, my father was out of town, but returning that same afternoon. Ella, my mother, gave me $12.00. "He paid for your college education, private flight classes, and plane ticket to California. He loves you, yet fearful you might fail," she said, hugging me. I kissed her sweet cheeks, because I knew my grandparents were an upper-class colored family in Virginia, and she married the lower-class James Duke Smith. The Sapphos threatened to disown her. We lived middle class; mother professed my father was the sole provider of his family.

As soon as I landed in Sacramento, a downpour hit. I didn't care; I was too busy hoping for a hot meal. I stepped off the plane and thought of my mother. I didn't estimate how hard it would be to say goodbye to her. She stayed in my room, weeping, and found a bit of Ella Fitzgerald's smile.

She packed a whole fried chicken and biscuits for me to eat on the plane. Right at the airport, I ate every morsel. Eight and half hours later, I wished I had saved at least a chicken breast to carry me to Sacramento. I was in line waiting—twenty men behind me, ten in front, and another one stood next to me.

"Man, it's cold out here," Handsome Joe said, lighting a Marlboro cigarette. He puffed, blew the smoke in my direction. His hazel eyes looked at my black eyes. "This feels like New York, my friend, not California. What the hell are they doing up there?" He then dropped his cigarette, placed his left, shivering hand in his pocket. The right hand he extended to me. "Yeah, my name is Handsome Joe. Nice to meet you. Listen, if the lieutenant says anything about smelling smoke, pretend you don't smell anything, didn't see anything, and definitely don't say a damn thing." He lit another cigarette. "This stuff is the only thing to keep me warm, and every day I say I'm gonna quit, but I have a pack just in case I change my mind. Now I know I will never quit if I got to fly airplanes in another country at that. Shit, I know in Europe everybody smokes. So what the fuck is your name anyway?"

"John Smith to you Handsome Joe," I said. "Or should I call you Smoking Joe?"

Several hours passed, at evening meal, Handsome Joe and I sat together. "What a difference a hot meal makes," Handsome Joe said. He reached for another slice of white bread. I was sick in the stomach from the chicken soup. The lieutenant announced it was lunch and dinner until everyone was checked-in and ready for training tomorrow at 0600.

I walked outside; Handsome Joe followed me. He dropped a cigarette on the ground. The lieutenant ran passed us.

"I think it's time to quit smoking, Handsome Joe," I said, glancing at his cigarette. I grabbed it.

"Yeah, thanks for the advice friend," he said. "I'm gonna quit tomorrow after dinner." He snatched it swiftly out of my hands.

Strolling to my bunkroom, I lied down, thinking about my father. He was a heavy smoker. My mother was afraid he would forget to put out his cigarette and burn down the house. She never could sleep unless she was assured his eyes remained shut. I missed the sweet sounds of Ella's spirituals throughout our home.

"What you thinking about John?" Handsome Joe asked.

"Just thinking about home, Joe," I said.

"Home," Joe chuckled. "Well home is where the heart is and right now, you best leave home alone, and get some sleep. Home—what's that? I been homeless all my life."

I didn't say a word, because Ella's voice was singing: "Swing Low Sweet Chariot, Come to Carry me Home, Swing Low Sweet Chariot, Come to Carry me Home, I look over yonder and what do I see," and I drove off to sleep.

I thought I was having a nightmare, until the lieutenant's voice screamed in my ear. "Boy get up. Did you hear the bell?"

"No sir, I thought it was thunder, sir."

"Well boy, thunder you'll see if you don't get dressed, get out, and in formation right now." I rushed out and everybody started laughing.

"I tried to wake you up," Handsome Joe said. "But you were out. I said let him be; he was home."

"Yeah, I was home, and I guess you were right, that home is here and now."

"No, friend, home is staying awake before the lieutenant dropped you off at the gate."

I understood and looked at Handsome Joe with new respect.

The following day, we were introduced to Captain Bull Brown. He was a broad and musky, muscular man with a grey mustache. He said sternly, "I am in charge of your basic and advanced pilot training for the United States Air Force. Even though you may be of Negro descent, this is not a segregated Negro unit. On July 26, 1948, the Executive Order 9981 by President Harry Truman officially ended racial segregation in the Armed Forces.

"How far anyone goes depends upon your own ability. If you complete your training, test well, and received high evaluation in all maneuvers, you will have the skills and qualifications to become an airman." His short and strong presence recited the rules of the day. "Now men, if you have never been told you are a man, I am here to tell you, you are a man and may become a fierce pilot. Each of you is college educated, and has the opportunity to become an officer. But first, you must show me you are ready in every aspect of your training to move further along.

"The United States Air Force will enhance your ability to use your expertise and skills as a military fighter and leader in a unit of your own one day. That's of course, if you can make it, and if you can prove you deserve to be in the uniform. We demand discipline, a high degree of intelligence, and determination from you to accomplish your mission. This morning, and as long as you have the honor to serve in our uniform, I see soldiers. I am your superior, and while I am your superior, you do what I command first, second, and always.

"The year is 1949, the month is January, and you know you are the property of the United States of America. Not your momma, papa, Army or Navy, but the Air Force of the United States of America. The Air Force is your parent; your family is the man who stands on your left. The man on your right is your brother, as well as the man in front of you. Look at each other as brothers, as family, as men, here to honor your country. Make your other family proud, and that other family is me.

"To make me proud, you must listen and learn about your enemy, about who you will be trained to fight, kill, and bring victory to your brother, your family, the Air Force of the United States of America. All right, I'm going to tell you a story, and when you are old and very gray, you will be able to tell this story for the rest of your life. It starts from the beginning; the beginning was the United States of America." My eyes were bright and big, and every eye was on Captain Bull Brown, especially Handsome Joe.

Pilot training at Mather Air Force Base was intense and thrilling in first month, and throughout the eight months I was there. I excelled in military tactics, maneuvers, and, in my F-51 pistol plane, I managed to execute a "positive G" performance in rapid turning movements in a dogfight. My instincts and intense training equipped my body from the danger of downward flow of blood that could bring about the end to a pilot's life, a blackout. Handsome Joe's sharpness was behind me, and we became friends. Officers noticed we worked well together, and we were on the top of our game. One Friday after midnight, Joe went for a smoke, and I made the mistake to follow him. Captain Brown spotted us near an unrestricted area, and ordered us both in detention. Joe was smoking near unmarked crates of ammunition; Captain Brown said "You boys are bit cocky that you would jeopardize the entire base. No pilot training this weekend, you will be working chores for me." Saturday morning at 0500, our materials were two buckets of water, soap, and two ripped rags to wash General Steel Haynes' jeep.

We were stationed behind the detention building until Captain Brown inspected our work and informed us whether or not the jeep was clean. Four hours later, the sun was blistering and bouncing on my lower back. I stopped to rest for a moment, and Handsome Joe picked up the bucket of cold water and splashed it on my back. "What the hell are you doing? Are you a fool? Do want the captain to keep us out here for another four hours? You know he is watching us, and you stop to take a break." I bent down to grab a rag, and my back pain was killing me. "I need to rest for a minute."

"Now who's fooling who friend?" Handsome Joe said.

In a flash, we heard. "You boys having fun out here, I see." Captain Bull Brown said. His black oxfords pointing in between Joe and me.

"No sir," Joe said. "We were trying to cool off a bit, that's all."

Swarthy eyes stared at me. "Son, is that right?" Captain said. "Are you trying to cool off?"

"No sir, no sir," I said. "We were giving your jeep another rinse before we shine and make it sparkling clean, sir."

"Is that right?" Captain Brown asked. Gazing at his oxford's shoes, he said, "Well, then boys, I could use a shine right on my shoes." I looked at Joe who moved in a step closer to Captain Brown and jumped in front of Joe.

"Yes sir. Do you want a shine now or after we finish shining your jeep, sir?" I asked urgently.

He placed his right hand in his pocket, pulled out a gold watch. "Now, let's see, it should take you boys another hour to shine the captain's jeep, and when it's sparkling brighter than my gold watch, you can pick up my shoes and buff them." Captain Brown examined the jeep. "She is definitely standing taller; Sunday you will have the pleasure of washing Admiral's Blanchester's jeep."

"Yes sir, yes sir," I said. He turned and locked his eyes on Joe.

"Yes, sir," Handsome Joe said lackadaisically.

The sun popped off Captain Bull Brown's gold watched. "You see this watch? I shine it every day, and starting today, my shoes are to be shined every day." We observed how Captain Brown slowly placed his gold watch back in his pocket.

In unison, we saluted. "Yes sir, captain," we said.

As soon as the captain walked away, Joe said, "I overheard some guys talking about Captain Brown, somebody said he was in the 333rd Field Artillery Battalion. What do you think John...the captain a hero?"

I was dead-silent. And then suddenly, I took another look at Captain Brown. "Man, I would give anything for a smoke." Joe said bluntly.

I was redder than my great-grandfather's Greek ears. "You would want a cigarette which is why we are here in the first place. The second place is this weekend, scrubbing and shinning the captain's jeep, tomorrow is the admiral's jeep. Friday before midnight, I was an aviator."

Joe faced me, clenched his fists. "I said at 1200:01 how bad I felt that you were thrown in detention with me. I ain't gonna tell you again. You don't see tears falling down my chest, and cigarettes ain't in me anymore. But I can still remember how good it feels to taste that Marlboro in my mouth and your complaining can't make me stop."

I squeezed the rag in the cold dirty water, and began scrubbing the jeep. "Cigarettes are your problem, washing and shining is my problem, but not for long." My fist was tight and I was ready to fight.

At once, Joe grabbed his white rag. "Don't you worry John; we will be out of here and back where we belong."

12

Saturday night, Joe and I were back in the cell, and it was blue-black hell. I could not sleep, and Joe would not allow me to, because at 2300 hours, I was stuck listening to his sleep talk.

"I knew in my heart she was trouble, but I couldn't help myself," he said again and again, and then kept mumbling to himself. I thought about Captain Brown's extolling the virtues of being an excellent soldier and how Joe and I were letting our brothers down.

Minutes past, and soon it was Sunday at 0400 hours. I had no sleep. I was anxious about the captain marching in with more chores. I looked at my watch and Joe pacing back and forth. He plopped to the gritty concrete floor. "Suzy Mae," he mumbled, moments later, eyes shut.

Yeah, I wanted to hate him for my current situation. Still, I never had seen Joe like this before. He always said he had no family, now he is out of his mind over a woman name Suzy Mae.

Though it felt like hours had passed, soon, Handsome Joe's back was against the stone wall, reaching in his front pocket for a cigarette. "Damn," he said. "The captain took my matches."

"Joe, what the heck are you doing?"

"Man, will you be quiet and stop talking to me—I'm remembering. I don't want to lose her again."

"What's with you, Joe? Captain said we will be out of here on Monday, and you can't sleep." Joe was tearful, with his arms tight around his waist.

"What's wrong? Are you missing your home?"

Joe walked to the corner side of our dwarfish space and coughed. "Even when I don't have a smoke, I still feel like I'm smoking." He smiled.

"Are you thinking about your family?"

"Man didn't I tell you I didn't have a family; I didn't have a home, I didn't have a damn dime, which is how I got into joining this place in the first place."

"Yeah, but you said you didn't want to lose her again. Is 'her' your mother?"

"Man, how can she be my momma, if I never had a momma?"

"Well, all I know is you better stop smoking before both of us are put out of the only home you ever had, and now the home I have." Joe nodded, dropped his cigarette.

His eyes were dry. He danced around looking up at the stars in between the black steel bars. He circled around and steeply squatted next to me. "Look I was attending college at City University and sharing a room with some other guys from school on 139th Street. At night I worked at a numbers joint on 125th and 8th Avenue. Every morning, and I mean every morning, before class I stopped to have breakfast at Ideal Restaurant on 145th Street and Lenox Avenue.

I'm sitting at the counter, smelling the best grits, red sausages, and fried fish your mouth could eat. Man, for twenty-five cents, you could get you a meal for the day, and if I had a family—home—well friend, Ideal Restaurant was it. Except this Friday morning, I had no money, since I lost it playing cards the night before. I could only afford coffee; I was hungry until I looked up and saw a surprise: a new girl. She was a woman, built; perfect the way I like a woman to be. And I was thinking—that woman could make me stop smoking. I first saw her earlobes. She was waiting tables. Guys looked at her, and she looked at me. Our eyes met, and she stared at my mouth. Her hair was pulled back in a curly pony tail. Her ear lobes were longing, lusting for me. A man could not help but to want her body; she had pink freckles wherever she allowed your eyes to see. Her uniform gave you a peek at the pleasure of her perky breast. I was on my third cup of coffee, no more money, and I could not leave.

She walked to my seat. "May, I help you? Would you like anything else?"

I put both my hands together like I was praying in a Holy Ghost church. "I was hoping to get your name, and then I would pay my bill and leave."

She didn't think that was funny. "Your bill is fifteen cents for three cups of coffee, sir."

Politely, I said "Ah, where you from Miss, not from New York?"

She wiped the table. "No sir."

"So, what's a nice Irish girl like you doing working her?" She started to walk away. "Okay, I'll leave you alone; just tell me your name." She moved away. I sat there, and lit a cigarette. She came back, and gave me my bill. So, I said. "Excuse, me Miss, could I add another cup of coffee?"

"Sir, I would have to make another pot of fresh coffee, and give you another bill."

I lit another cigarette. "Look, I would leave if you just tell me your name." She is driving me crazy, but I'm not showing it. I'm sitting, being cool, and looking at her earlobes. Moments flew by, she approaches, her pecan frost nails held my bill, and she bends over.

"Maybe, I don't want you to leave."

Man, I fell out of my chair, laughter exploded, the manager scurries over. "Handsome Joe, do you want anything else?"

I bounce right up, still thinking I'm being cool. She hands me a white slip, strolls to the cash register. I lay my money on the counter. Her back is facing another customer. I'm staring at her sexy self. I leave, walk toward St. Nicholas Park. I glare at the bill. "What the fuck," I said. She wrote her name and telephone number in red ink with a big quotation mark "Suzy Mae." By that time, I got to 135th Street, I ran up the one hundred and thirty-two steps in St. Nicholas Park, screaming her name, dreaming about her touch. Sitting in my political science class, I only thought of Suzy Mae. I didn't want a cigarette, I wanted to start at her earlobes, and love her everywhere else."

We fell in love, and we were together every night the month of January 1944. At the same time, I enrolled in the Civilian Pilot Training Program at my school. At first it was a joke, I told myself, you know, you don't like the prerequisite of mandatory enlistment in the Air Force. But Suzy said. "You're smart," and you talk about airplanes when you're not smoking cigarettes." We laughed, and I loved her real good that night.

Even so, when my instructor mentioned that a Negro woman named Willa Brown earned her private pilot's license in 1938. I mean, right then, I said, "If she can do it, why the fuck can't I." I rolled on my stomach, she rolled on top. I kept thinking about Willa Brown. "Joe, let me pay for your training," Suzy said, and I did. This is before I realized, she had another man on the road with the Duke Ellington band.

Things were going too good: I was doing well in school, training to become an aviator, and in love.

A week before, I saw her last. She tells me Cecil is returning from a gig in Paris. I found out this dude brought her from Louisiana, pays people to watch her while he is traveling. She lived on a parlor floor in a brownstone on 137th Street.

The morning I was running late for my physics class, we kissed and planned to meet at Small Paradise on 135th Street. Suzy Mae never showed up. I stopped by her place, the landlord said her man came with his trombone, and they moved out. I gave him fifty cents, and he told me she went on tour with him in Brazil. That was four years ago, and yet, luck was on my side. Because, I graduated, and had a place to go: a one way ticket to Sacramento, baby. I can't stop thinking of her. She hated cigarettes, and that was the only 'no' I said to her. As much as I loved Suzy, I refused to give up the Camel."

"Joe, how did you start to smoke anyway?" I asked quickly.

"None of your fucking business," he said fierily. "What the hell, my uncle Willie Manchester turned me into smoking at thirteen in 1939. We were staying at the Harriet Hotel and Extensions on 127th Street and St. Nicholas Avenue. The rate were $4.00 weekly, and nightly Uncle Willie hustled numbers at the Red Rooster Bar and Grill on 141st Street. A pack of Camels was on the night stand, and he practically forced one in my mouth, telling me, "Joe, it's like this. I'm your only family you got, and I don't have time to raise a child. You might as well smoke like me, caused I ain't stopping."

He would come to our room drunk from drinking Foxwood Whisky; he smelled bad, looked bad, and mad as hell when he lost money. I never got into drinking like him; but, I fell in love with Camel cigarettes.

I was always smart, and don't ask me where I got it. I was going to high school on 140th Street and St. Nicholas Avenue. Once, a bolt of lightning hit the hotel, liquor had him screaming. He lay down scared out of his mind. "Joe, I been watching you; you really smart. I never learned how to read, and how the fuck did you? I fantasized of flying airplanes when I was younger than you. I saw this magazine cover with a man dressed up in leather jacket, boots, and hat, standing strong next to an airplane; the title read, *Aviator*, and thought, damn, I want to be that."

Some Saturday nights after Willie lost his gambling money, he and I would go to the hilltop at St. Nicholas Park. He takes out his revolver, shoots at the airplanes in the sky. Willie Man was sick every day. I have to give him credit, he convinced me to go to college.

He said, "Joe you ain't gonna have your good looks forever. It won't last long; look at me."

"Willie Man, how can I go to college, we barely can eat."

"I ain't talking about money, Handsome Joe; you don't need money to go here."

"What the fuck you talking about?" I told him, "You drunk, not me."

"Joe, we sitting on the gray hard grounds of City College of New York, it's free." Then, he put his revolver in his coat pocket, and directed both hands to the sky. "Look up at the stars in the sky; it's the only real peace I know."

I knew, but didn't see, and a month later, he died from a severe heart attack. I buried him; nobody came to the funeral. I was alone, moved to a row house on 139th and 8th Avenue. I hustled at nights at the Red Rooster; mornings ran the hill in St. Nicholas Park to my classes at City College.

There was a long silence. Then I said. "Joe, why do you say you were homeless? You had a home in New York."

"Man, what do you think a home is? It more than a bed to lie in—it's a family. Uncle Willie told me he spent sixteen years in Rikers Island, and when he got out, he had no family. He went to visit friends down south, returned to New York City with me. Suzy Mae and my uncle were my family. They both are gone."

At 0500 Joe was asleep, and I could not sleep. I thought about Captain Brown, and "what was his true purpose? He's been recording our success from day one. Other guys smoke, and he smokes, but we made a stupid mistake. The mistake I made was becoming Joe's friend, and now his baby sitter. "I said to myself, there can't be another mistake, because, I don't need a friend. The price of our friendship is too high, and I am not the guardian."

When I was five, I asked my mother for a little brother. She said, "Your father said we can't afford another child." He didn't care how much money my mother inherited. He was not going to touch her money. She cried, and I never asked her again. I got to make my own way, except for my mother; I too don't have a family. I was determined to succeed in the Air Force, and become military pilot.

The pavement floor felt like rotten, hardened dirt. We had no cots—just walls and bars. I could see guys lining in formation; preparing to climb into F-82 Twin Mustangs. I stared at Joe's sleeping position: arms served as pillows, right big toe held his cigarette. I walked over to wake him, leaned, and said, "What's that lying next to him?" Pages of brown paper had fallen out of his pocket. Two steps closer, I gazed at a letter written in blue ink. I thought, "If I wake him up now, he will think I saw his letter." And without thinking, I instantly grabbed the paper.

With Joe's letter, I stood next to the rustic and molded window bars. It was dated August 7, 1939.

W. D. Moore

Dear Son, my name is Margaret Josephine Spice, but all my life, I have been Baby Doll. I am your momma, and before you throw this letter away, I pray you read it one day. In 1914, I was seventeen, and a singer with a blues band in Jackson, Mississippi. I never had a singer's voice, but the band leader, Joseph, hired me anyway, because he said "you look like a baby doll, and if you don't bring in paying customers, nobody will." And so, I was singing with the Joes Blue Bumping Band, and after midnight, I was the lover to the saxophone player, Joseph. I now realize I was ill, because I could not resist him. I would do anything he told me to do. Every time we played throughout the early morning sun, he would grab me around my waist and carry me upstairs to our single room.

I sat on the bed, watched him take off his clothes and then he said "open them wide, much wider this time, and I laid down on the bed, listening to the broken spring board, and his singing in my ear "Baby Doll, Baby Doll, you don't know what you got, and I don't care, cause I got it, I got it." On June 10, I felt funny down there, and I said "Joe when you gonna marry me sugar," and he laughed and said "What we need to get married for, we together ain't we?"

I rolled off the month-old sheet and said "cause I'm pregnant, and I want to settle down." He came over and gently touched my mouth, and said "Margaret, how do I know, it's mine." He walked to the mirror, bushed his oily black hair and said "Baby Doll, shit everybody wants Baby Doll, I guess, you be wanting a baby too!" Then he stood over me and said "Tonight, wear your tight satin red dress showing your sexy long legs. I wrote a nice song for you call "Red Baby Blues."

Son, I had no place to go. He stayed with me until I was four months pregnant, and left me alone in Juniors Joint, after I finished my last song. He didn't come back to our room, and the next morning I found an envelope with a $5.00 bill, and a note said "Sorry Baby Doll, got to move on." After crying for two months, Junior let me stay, working behind the bar until you were born.

A year later, 1915, I was still good-looking, and men didn't care if you were next to me sitting on my hips, just as long as they could see my legs, and longing for my lips. This went on for another year, until the owner said "Margaret, you got to go. I hired a single girl here. We left and took a bus to my momma's home in Baton Rouge, Louisiana.

My Momma, Miss Lucy or Lady Luck, depending on if she made money from the numbers that day, saw you and said "if that ain't the prettiest, handsome child my eyes have ever seen. She instantly fell in love with you. My momma loved you more than she ever loved me, and she said, "The only reason, you can stay here is because of my grand-son." I started getting jealous of you and tired of people telling me how handsome you were. Two years later when I saw a billboard downtown that read "Joe's Blue Bumping

Band" in town for one night at Sam's Shell Joint I knew I was going to see your daddy again.

I wore my tight red satin dress, and that night, Joe was playing "No Blues for You." I walked in and sat at a single table. Everybody's eyes were on me, except for Joe's. Joe pretended he did not see me, but when the set was finished, he came over to my table, and grabbed my hand, and threw me in the bathroom, and said "open them Baby Doll legs." I pulled up my dress and spread my legs, and he lunged right in and whispered "Margaret, you so wet." I said "I've been saving it for you." The next day, I forgot about you and my momma, and left with him. A year later, he dropped me in an unknown town. I said, never again, and I went back to get you, and found out my momma had died.

When, I asked for you, no one knew where you were. I was told that you were passed around from family member to family member until there was no family. For months and months I searched for you, but no one remembered my son.

Now, I'm thirty-six, and I will never stop searching for you. I have no family but you.

I was told my momma's man took her money and Handsome Joe. They went up north to New York, and Willie Manchester was working in a Row House playing numbers on 125th Street. People talk all the time, so I didn't pay it no mind, until you were seventeen. Willie wrote me a letter asking for money to feed my son.

I sent money, and was told Willie was dead, and you were gone. I don't know if you will get my letter, open my letter, or read my letter, but I must write to you Baby, I must.

Weakness is a working nightmare that gives you twenty-four hours of pain. It slips up and seeps in your soul. Somehow, you find the courage to say no.

I crawled and cared about something more than your daddy. I found you. I love you Handsome Joe, my son. Your momma, Margaret.

I stared at my friend. Tip-toed to Joe and placed his letter next to his pants pocket.

That early Monday morning, July 1950, Captain Bull Brown's shiny oxfords came bursting in the brig. "You boys got advanced training on the F-51 pistol plane. I don't' have to tell you; you will have to work around the clock; and If I see one more foolish mistake you both are out. You both been assigned to Korea. Let's go—there's a damn war."

"Yes, sir," Joe said. He was alert, awake. I smiled at Joe. "What you smiling about?" Captain Brown yelled.

"Nothing, sir," I said cheerfully.

"It better be something like marching out," he said, nodding his head.

"Yes, sir," I said.

Joe reached for his cigarette. He looked at his letter, and gazed at me. He put his hands on his letter and into his shirt pocket.

"Joe, we got to go," I said, standing behind Captain Brown.

"Moving out," Captain Brown shouted.

"You know, friend," Joe grinned. "I think sleeping and smoking don't work for me anymore. He flipped his cigarette on the ground and charged briskly passed me.

13

It would require a bucket of water to wake John from his bottomless sleep at Hotel Cesare', because he dived back to Korea in 1950.

"Strong coffee was what Handsome Joe and I needed when we arrived at Kimpo Air Field at 1000 hours in October. We were two Negro pilots assigned to the 455th Squadron. It was bone chilling. Our commanding Officer, J.V. Pitts, said, "Drop your bags, and report to the ready room at 0100."

Walking to the tents, we stopped to stare at the F-82 Twin Mustangs lined up. Three older pilots glared at our gabardine wool jackets, khaki pants, and an insignia on the right sleeve that showed our ranks as second lieutenants. Three younger pilots ran passed by, and a captain who resembled Cary Grant shouted "Hey Butter Bars." I saluted, noticed his light flying suit, flight jacket, and Joe saluted, observing his paratrooper boots. We both eyed his leather gloves holding a white, hard flying helmet.

Six fighter pilots launched their Mustangs and taxied off, gearing up for their high-noon dogfight mission. The blistering wind seeped into my soul, and it seemed my skin peeled off. I gazed at the red bold sun, the F-82s flying north, and suddenly their wings whipped 30,000 feet above the whitest clouds I had ever seen. Joe readjusted his garrison cap, and said, "It's cold out here brother." I put my ashy hands quickly in my two front pockets, and said, "Yeah."

The tent's temperature was 40° and ten degrees warmer than outside; there was an oil stove, but no oil. Newly polished shoes jumped on the hard, wooden floor, and I said, "This is the only resemblance of a house." Joe dropped his sleeping bag in the center, sat on top, and said, "Speak for yourself." And yet, we were where we wanted to be. No complaints, and confident in the purpose of the new day.

One month later was a decade, especially the day of November 13, 1950. I was waiting to venture to the communist black-blue sea. I thought, "I know, I should not be afraid, and I think, I am not, until I can't sleep. The chill hovers in this tent, but in my cockpit, my tight G-suit, my past fear leaves me, and my eyes are focused like a snake.

This is the life I live day by day, and if I am lucky, the next moment will bring me home before moonlight. Handsome Joe relishes the hunt and being hunted. We fly in the same rhythm, and even when he tries to move in closer, he follows my direction every time. He smells the enemy before I activate my machine guns, and the aerial combat begins. Yesterday we returned back alive.

Bobby Jack was married, I heard. Wonder what she will do, now that her man is gone? I don't think I will get married—for what, if our lives are never long?

I hopped out of the sleeping bag, and was ready to report to the ready room. It was 0200:45 hours, Handsome Joe's paratroopers boots were laid neatly above his head, and his coat on top. I slept with my coat on. As wingman, Joe only requires his camel cigarettes to keep him warm.

"Joe, get up, it's time to go." He turns over to his right side away from my boots. "I'll meet you in the commander's room—it's freezing, and I can't wait for another ten minutes."

Handsome Joe immediately sits straight up. "You would leave me, wouldn't you?" He jumped up and grabbed his boots and said, "Man it's chilly, but not colder than when I was twenty, and a young thing sneaked me in when her parents were visiting folks in Orangeburg, South Carolina. I over slept and rushed down the third floor. Her parents and luggage were at the door as I was leaving. They did not move; the old lady stared at my corduroy pants, polyester sweater, and a borrowed, stolen, black-leather jacket from my room-mate, Puckeye. The father wrangled with their bags and looked at my zip up half-boots in the bitter cold that were unzipped. His face was blacker than my jacket—he wore a long white wool coat. She walked inside their building, but he watched me until I turned on 121st Street. I kept moving, holding on to my switch blade."

I laughed, and loosen up somewhat, and stepped out the tent. "How do you sleep without your coat on?" I asked Joe.

"John, I don't care if it's zero, I can't sleep with too many clothes on my body. I been this way all my life, from New York to this hell-hole Korea. As soon as this war is over, I am finding my woman; I won't need to wear clothes to bed."

"You see that lonely star? That's the only woman I care about. If I can keep my eyes on her light, I can find my way back home. For me, flying will always be my first love. She is everything, and I don't miss anything."

"Yeah, you say, because, you have not found her yet."

I groped the commander's door. "Yeah, well that day is not here, and all I now want is my Mustang."

Exactly at 0255, Joe and I slipped in and found our usual spot in the ready room. Commander Pitts was speaking to eight other fighter pilots; he glared at his watch and continued drinking his black coffee in a tarnished canteen cup. He placed his cup down, coughed hard from his chest, and tightened his wool black scarf around his broad cutthroat neck.

Commander Pitts spoke plain and explained the mission, "Bobby Jack and Tex Rod were mixing it up with four MiGs at 22,000 feet patrolling along the Yalu River before they were eliminated. These damn aerial shots don't give us the exact location, but close enough to know where you can roll and run them out of the sky. The MiG pilots were lucky yesterday, but our air-to-air gunnery will out maneuver them, because every man in here is an exceptional killer." Sweat poured down his forehead frown lines; droplets of moisture fell through two semicircle holes in his left ear, and slowed down exactly on his crew cut-neck. He unwrapped his scarf, coughed, sipped his coffee and said "This is a bloody business; we seek our enemy, kill him, and come back home. I don't want any wingman over-stepping his leader." He looked directly at Handsome Joe. "I don't want any leader to lose his focus for a second." He looked at me. "Again, men," he said. "Your eyes are your weapon, hunger is your heart, and gunnery closes the deal.

"Every man in here can become an ace, and some of you already are on your way. I became an ace in the Second World War, not by worrying about making five kills. When you do, you become carless, and dead. This "Civil War" is not ending this morning. You have time to make history. Just eat the bloodied meat one steak at a time. Each team is clear on your assignment and knows what to do. That's all; report back to the base at 0600."

Five bands of two, ten F-82 Twin Mustang pilots climbed in their cockpits, and fifteen minutes later reached an altitude above 20,000 feet. The temperature dropped to below zero degrees, the winds pounded on the wings, and the planes motioned with might when they dispersed to pursue their own dogfight.

Handsome Joe and I directed our Mustangs to the Yalu River at Chosan. Exactly at 0500, I spoke to Joe on his radio. "I see red."

"Are you sure, how do you know?"

"When he is dead," I said. "Stay with me Joe, I see red."

"I don't see red, John."

"Keep with me Joe; I see red."

Commander Pitts screamed on the radio, "If the leader says he sees red, he sees red."

"Yes, sir," Joe said.

I was rolling at 21,000 feet and dipped to 18,000 and on a hot pursuit with a MiG-15. Joe was swinging above at 19,000 steady above the quiet black sea. I searched for the target, keeping my hands firm on six .50-caliber machine guns when Joe made a sharp swirl down to 16,000 feet. Instantly I saw the tail-end of a MiG-15 pilot rotating in his direction at 15,000 feet.

"Joe, I see red, at fifteen and heading at sixteen." Joe speeded down to 15,500 feet, and he still did not see the Chinese pilot, and I said, "black tail is black."

I remained at 16,000, and seconds later dropped to 15,000 feet, and no longer saw my target. It was 0600, and my stomach felt hungry, and in a split second, I saw breakfast. "Joe, I see red; he is deep at 13,000." I pursued, pointed, and fired. I saw the burning enemy aircraft. "It's a dead body that's cooling." Three seconds later, I hijacked to 20,000 feet, and Joe steam-rolled to 21,000 feet.

"Was that hit our breakfast or lunch?" Joe asked.

"That was breakfast, baby, it's too damn early for lunch. We will soon have company on our tail."

"How is your fuel, John?"

"I got more than I need for another kill." At 0900, and five hours later, we searched for juicier red meat. My eyes moved with the white clouds in the sky at 30,000 feet. I was in control, confident, and lusting for blood.

It was 1100 when Joe and I returned to Kimpo Airfield. The cold had left my body; we walked into the commander's hut. He was eating lunch and drinking bland, black coffee. "Every officer that was not dead heard you men; the ready room was loud and proud, and it's clear you can dogfight. You men performed your jobs like professional soldiers out there." He hesitated, "You know, I ask the same for all my men? Can you fight, come back, and fight again?"

Joe gawked at his powdered eggs, and the commander said, "get some food, and be in the ready room at 0300. That's all."

"Yes, sir," We walked out. "When I pick up my C-rations, I am going to pretend I'm eating steak and real eggs," Joe said.

"I will pretend I am drinking strong coffee from Chile."

"I changed my mind," Joe said. "I think I'll pretend I'm eating fried pork chops, gravy, and burnt onions on top."

Later that night, Joe was outside the tent smoking a Camel cigarette, and sitting on a hard wooden box. It was 1900, and I stepped out and looked at the sky. "I don't see her tonight; she's gone," I said.

"Here, take a taste of my Camel," Joe replied. "You smoke like a pro brother."

"Yeah, my father smoked every day," I said. "It's probably in my blood, and why I hate it."

"Well, look up. Do you see her now?"

"No," I said.

Joe smiled. "I think of my woman when I smoke; her body is in me. Have you ever had a woman?"

"No, not like the way you love your woman. I liked a girl in college, her name was Camilla; she was dark chocolate and tasted better than ice cream. She wanted to get married, but I refused to fall in love with her. I couldn't let her get in my way of becoming an aviator. She said I broke her heart, and I said I don't have a heart; I had to move on."

I handed Joe back his cigarette, and Joe pulled a letter from his back pocket. "Here, this is my momma's letter you read. I want you to hold it for me. I tell you John, the way you took care of that red pilot today, I know you gonna make it out here."

"What about you?"

"Shit, I'm making it too, but you just my insurance policy."

I wandered back in my tent, laid on the cot, and closed my eyes, but something was different this time. My stomach was quiet, and voices were not speaking about me. I relaxed and turned on my right side. "Maybe, I will live one more day."

Someone knocked at his door. John awoke drenched in sweat. He was back in Rome, Italy, New Year's Eve, 1972.

"Shit, am I having a heart attack?" He pushed the wet blanket off his body, jumped into the rustic shower, and no hot water. The cool water soothed his brain and body. "Colder, baby," he screamed. The water gave him a chilled pleasure. "Some guys just can never get the Hotel Cesar's charm." He laughed boisterously.

14

When John raced down the cast iron stairway, the manager greeted him. "Ciao," he said, dazed at his pristine uniform.

"I need to make an international call to the United States," John said." From nowhere, his head was throbbing, his throat was thirsty, and his ears tightened anticipating her voice. The telephoned rang. John nodded to Hamilton who stopped to glance at the Italian magazine with Claudia Cardinale on the cover. Holding the telephone for several minutes, he made a note that it was eleven-fifteen her time. "It's early; where is she?" He slammed the phone. "She's given me a headache. I'll try again later."

Second Lieutenant Hamilton saluted John. "Sir, I knocked on your door earlier. Did you know this hotel does not have hot water? I spoke to the concierge and he said, "It's warm most mornings, then turned his head, and said something in Italian."

"My shower was warm Hamilton; perhaps, you didn't sing a song while enjoying the water."

"A song, sir. No, I could not think of any song, my body was feeling like bloodied hell, sir."

"Hamilton, you don't like smoke, cold showers, and your colonel's coffee. Why did you become an officer in the Air Force?"

"Because, sir, I love being an aviator, and I wanted to travel around the world, sir."

"Hamilton, this is the world, get used to it or find another day job. Let's go, I'm hungry."

"Sir, can you believe in five hours, it will be 1973?"

"No, I'm thinking in twenty-four hours we will be flying home, and I will be in bed with my wife."

"Sir, I don't have a sweetheart, but tonight, if I meet her, I hope her shower is hot."

"Hamilton, she may have something hotter than water, and ways to help you beg for cold." Hamilton became silent, lifted his coat collar close to his ears. They walked for two more blocks. "Sofia Street has changed," John said.

"Let's turn onto Rosa Street." He saw a sign that read "Café Rosa." Two young ladies were seated in the window. They giggled at Hamilton.

"Sir, what about this place?" Hamilton said, smiling at the ladies. And they stepped inside the ornate wooden door.

"Table for two?" the waitress asked. "Or four?" she looked at the ladies' table.

"A table for two, please," John said. Hamilton frowned.

"We have six tables and only two are available: one near the window, and the other in the rear, closer to the back."

"We prefer the table in the back." John led, Hamilton paced slowly behind him. The waitress handed them a four by seven menu and said, "Should I bring champagne for the New Year?"

"Yes," Hamilton said. "Could you send a glass of champagne to those two ladies?"

The waitress' eyes were focused on John. "Champagne for you sir?" she asked.

"I prefer coffee, and strong."

"We have the best coffee in Rome, and it is always strong. I shall return to take your dinner orders."

A round loaf of *pane casereccio* was on the table. John cut himself half.

"Sir, it's New Year's Eve and you are drinking coffee."

"Hamilton, it's your first night here and you are spending your money on champagne."

The waitress carried champagne to the ladies' table. They waved to Hamilton. "Sir, may I go over and say hello?"

"Remember, tomorrow morning, we have to be at the base at 0700. Do you know where the base is, and how to get back to the hotel? If you are not at the base on time, you will be disciplined."

"Sir, I just want to say hello, I'll be back." Hamilton bumped into the waitress, and she almost spilled the coffee on her blouse.

"Excuse me, Miss. I'm sorry," Hamilton said and scurried to the ladies' table.

John assisted her with the tray. "I apologize for my lieutenant; he has never been to such a charming place as your café." John stared at Hamilton. "He's a bit of a child tonight."

She placed the champagne glass and the coffee on the table. Her eyes pierced at his. "I made the coffee very strong, and if you prefer it stronger, I can make it better for you."

He glared at her Asian eyes, thick, black eyelashes, and handsome smile. In his mind, "she is beautiful woman." He analyzed her body: she is wider in the hips than most Asian women I had seen in Korea. Everything else was Italian; in the way she spoke, the way she was, and yet, there was mystery."

With her arms on her ample hips, she laughed. "Your Lieutenant Child has just left with the ladies."

"My lieutenant is searching for a hot shower."

"On New Year's Eve, it seems he may have found two showers, don't you think?"

He stared at his watch. "Is this restaurant staying open late?" he asked subtly.

She poured his coffee in an artistic porcelain cup. "My restaurant closes tonight at eleven o' clock."

He smelled the satisfying aroma of his coffee. "Is this your restaurant? It's charming, and you were right; the coffee is strong." Her sable lips opened slightly to speak, but another customer raised his hand. She left John's table.

At eleven o'clock she wished her last two customers Happy New Year—except John. He stayed drinking champagne, eating Montasio cheese, and a bottle of white Arneis was near his reach. Half an hour later, she locked the door, dimmed the lights, and went to the bar. She returned to John's table, poured him a glass of Sangiovese and casually sat in a chair. He was soundless as she studied his hands slicing the cheese. Her dainty left hand held her full Roman face; her right hand sipped her Sangiovese. Suddenly her glass went to his mouth. She wiped his lip with a cloth napkin. "Thank you," he said. "What is your name?"

"Do you want to know my name or where I live?"

He thought, "I'm not too drunk to know I want this woman. There is something about her: in the way, she holds her body; in the way, her thick, black hair ends behind her ears; in the way her rosy lips move; in the way her short frame and small breasts are a blessing for her size. And the way, her behind bounces Megan's way." This acknowledgement brought goose bumps on his arms. He drank the last Arneis.

She remained behind the bar, pouring a bottle of Bordeaux in a carafe. Natalie recalled in her mind how often her tender Japanese mother warned her to stay away from Americans. I was girl of seventeen, and today, I am twenty-eight. Papa taught me how to take care of myself. On New Year's Eve, he walks in: tall, dark and handsome. I can feel he is not heartless. And tonight I want to pretend I am his heart."

She came back to him and set one wine glass on the table next to the carafe. "It's eleven-fifty; soon you will know my name." Her body moved in between his legs. He gripped her ambitious behind. She kissed him, unbuckling his metal belt buckle. The church bell rang at midnight. She opened her white lace blouse, raised her tight black shirt, and saddled on his thighs. "My name is Natalie." She unzipped his pants. John put himself perfectly there. "Harder, please," she said. And hard he did.

New Year's Day, he arouse in a twin-size bed with a triple-size headache. Two European pillows lay underneath his pulsating head. He glared at the nineteen-foot-high ceiling, glanced at the entire wall facing the bed of painted cupids. Glittering words read, "Amore, Cara mia, ti voglio bene." He grabbed his watch from the painted, green-leaf, oval glass table. It fell between the scattered eight, red-velvet, rectangular pillows. He snatched the watch, gazed at the time. It was 0500:30. He removed the white-linen embroidered blanket off his body.

"She is gone," John mumbled. "What is her name?" Immediately, she walked in naked, wearing high platform shoes. She held a nine-inch copper fry pan, and each foot closer, he smelled fresh peppers, mushrooms, onions, and eggs.

"Good morning," she said. John's head was pounding, his eyes transfixed to her breast. "I'm Natalie, John." She kissed him.

"Yes, Natalie, good morning," he smiled.

"This is a smoked-pancetta omelet, and after breakfast I'll make you a distinctive Italian lunch." She kissed him, her hand serenely held the fork. After, she finished feeding him, she place the pan on the floor.

"I have a headache," he said. "Do you have any aspirins?"

"Headache," Natalie enquired. Her body rested on top of his solid thighs and massaged his right and left temple. She kissed his forehead, ears, and neck. John was dazzled, in a dazed, and desired her *amore*. And when her red fingers pressed him in between his muscular legs, he grabbed her amiable rear, slid her inside. "Harder please," she whispered. He pushed harder and his headache was gone.

Exactly at six-fifteen that morning, he ascended to voices of laughter downstairs. He parachuted out of bed, peered at neatly pressed clothes, and polished shoes. His underpants were clean and on top of the copper fry pan.

He heard Natalie's voice conversing with customers—he quietly approached her. "Excuse me," he said. She smiled and moved away from her customers. "I'm leaving to go to the base. Thank you for a wonderful New Year's Eve."

Natalie touched his lips. "John, you have not had your coffee."

He removed her hand, kissed it. "I had strong coffee this morning. I must go; I can't be late."

"I'll see you later," she said.

He hailed a white taxi cab. She stood beside him. "Do you still have a headache?" John did not answer; the taxi arrived. He looked into her warm-hearted eyes. She closed the door. "I'll make you my mother's Italian dinner with spicy sweet sausages."

In the taxi John saw her waving and set his eyes back to his watch. He felt sick in the stomach and rubbed his chin. "I could use a shave." He needed her, missed her. "Megan, Baby, you're driving me crazy."

Colonel Rossini lounged in his chair, speaking to Second Lieutenant Hamilton, sipping his cappuccino. He checked the time. Another second passed; John watched Rossini through the glass door looking at his watch. "Captain, we have been waiting for you."

Second Lieutenant Hamilton saluted John. "Good morning sir."

John stared at the two cappuccinos in front of Hamilton. "I see Hamilton, you like coffee this morning."

"Yes, sir," Hamilton said.

"Good morning, Captain. The cappuccino is for you," Rossini said. John posed next to Hamilton. "Thank you, sir." Colonel Rossini walked to his door, closed it. "We have an urgent matter to discuss about your cargo, Captain. I have received new instructions from your superior. I am waiting for a call from Colonel Saddleback. Lieutenant Hamilton, please excuse us."

"Yes, sir," he said, saluting Rossini and John.

Colonel Rossini grabbed Hamilton's cappuccino. "Excuse, my manners Captain, Happy New Year. Did you find yourself warm this morning?" John eyes stared at Hamilton, who looked at his watch.

"Happy New Year sir," John replied. "Did I miss something this morning, sir?"

"Not at all Captain, you were ordered to report on duty at 0700 and you arrived five minutes early. He removed his eyeglasses and sneered. "Your second lieutenant informed me you were not in your hotel room this morning, so he reported in without you."

"What time did Hamilton report to the base, sir?"

Rossini frowned, wiped his eyeglasses, and faced John. "He was here ninety seconds before you arrived, Captain. You should know, never leave your lower-rank officer to be questioned about his superior's whereabouts. In any case, you have a larger concern; Colonel Saddleback will explain." Rossini glanced at his watch. "It is about 0600:59."

Vittorio knocked on the doctor. "Colonel, Colonel Saddleback's assistant telephoned and said the meeting has been postponed till tomorrow morning at 0600, sir."

"My coffee is cold," Rossini yelled.

"Sir, is there anything else, sir?" John asked.

"Yes, report back to the base at 0500 tomorrow. Your jet is refueled. I have never flown the Phantom, Captain. I am sixty-five years old. I might like to get in your cockpit, if I was not retiring. She is a beauty; you must be the best to carry such important cargo. Colonel Saddleback can't take any chances, Captain Smith." Rossini removed his eyeglasses, and settled in his lordly chair. "As a happily married man of forty-five years, I understand the fancies of soldiers from home, but I'm sure you are aware of such things. I suggest you and your lieutenant enjoy a fine, festive meal at Café Lucian; it happens to be my brothers' restaurant, and my assistant can give you the address."

Vittorio opened the door. "Sir, your coffee." He hurried out.

"Ah, this is indeed much better than at Café Rosa."

Their eyes stared sharper than Sir Lancelot's sword. Rossini put his eyeglasses back on. "Captain Smith, you may leave."

"Yes, sir." John's hand grasped the door.

"And Captain, my brother, Lucian, will treat you like family, but watch him: he will sit at your table, drink your wine, and double your bill."

"Thank you, sir." John opened the door. Rossini's eyes never wandered until he was gone.

Burning feet stormed past Hamilton, who moved briskly to keep steady with John outside in cool, chilled air.

"Second Lieutenant Hamilton, let's go and check on our girl; she must be lonely." The white and blue long-range supersonic jet controlled his calm.

John laughed, "Hamilton, let's go and have breakfast, before we report to duty tonight."

"Duty, sir? I thought we report in the morning, sir."

"No, we report at Café Lucian tonight at six o'clock and at the base tomorrow morning at 0500. John walked faster and in few seconds stopped. "Do you have a problem with my authority, Second Lieutenant Hamilton?"

"What? No, sir, Captain Smith."

"Should I suspect that you have a problem with my authority, Second Lieutenant Hamilton?"

"No sir, Captain Smith."

John's towering frame hit Hamilton the same. He thought of John Jr. "Son, never speak to another officer about your reporting officer's business. Did the colonel ask questions about my whereabouts, last night?"

"Yes, sir, and I told him we had dinner at Café Rosa."

"What else, Hamilton?"

"That's all, sir."

"Is that it, Hamilton?"

He saluted. "Yes sir, Captain Smith, sir," His misty eyes said.

Evening came. Café Lucian encompassed half of the block on Lucian Street. The other half was an herb shop name Lucian Leonardo. Sunny smiles seated in eight black tables, covered in white linen tablecloths with customers. Inside, the restaurant was spacious and elegant. At the doorway, the splendor was impressive: antique mirrors, marble tables, chandeliers, and pictures of famous Italian celebrities. John counted twenty tables, an array of headwaiters, sub-headwaiters, and waiters bursting throughout the restaurant like an Italian *balletto*. The smell of superb food was breathtaking, and John's nose bathed in hot chewy pagnotta. He wanted to dive in and take it off everyone's table. Hamilton spotted the girls. Customers and staff stared at one tanned and coca-tanned military athletic-looking men.

"Good evening," John said to the hostess. "I believe, we have reservations at six o'clock under the name Rossini. My name is Captain John Smith?"

"Yes, my uncle, Rossini, telephoned my papa, and said you were joining us for dinner. My name is Danielle. We have a reserved table for you—please follow me." Anxiously, Hamilton paced behind John who was restrained, observing the authentic grandeur of the room. Danielle, a girl of twenty, carried menus in her elegant tulips flawless hands. Her long pearls swirled as her beauty swept the parquet floor.

John and Hamilton walked side by side. "I think I found my sweetheart, sir," Hamilton said quietly—glancing at her silk stockings.

"Your headwaiter, Marcello, will serve you, and my papa will stop by shortly to officially welcome you," she said. "The red wine on the table is from our winery near Pordenone, the northeastern part of the Italy. I'm sure you will enjoy it…everybody does. Ciao," she said. She beamed and bounced to the front.

The label read: Rossini. John poured himself a glass and turned his attention to a short, stately man wearing a dark-blue pinstriped suit. His stale smile approached their table. "Gentlemen, gentlemen," Mr. Lucian said, reaching out his arm to shake their hands. They stood.

"Please sit down and enjoy my humble café. I am Lucian, and let me guess." He looked at John. "Captain Smith?"

John extended his hand. "Yes, and this is my friend, Second Lieutenant Hamilton." Hamilton grinned wide.

"This is a beautiful restaurant," John said.

"We like to think of Café Lucian as a small café experience with a big family celebration, but I thank you for the compliment." Suddenly, his head turned. "Where is Marcello?" He snapped his fingers twice and a young man of sixteen approached.

"Papa, I just stopped to…"

"No matter, Marcello, take care of our guests. They are friends of your uncle. Bring more wine and another wine glass for me. Tell the chef to prepare my special appetizers for the table." Marcello rushed.

"I apologize for my son—he is learning the business. He became lazy with four sisters pampering him. What about you, Captain Smith, do you have children?"

"Yes, I have a seventeen-year-old son, who attends college this September."

"Then you must understand," he sighed. John sipped his wine, and Lucian looked at Danielle. "I shall return to have a glass of wine with you, but now I want to make sure everything is perfect for your meal tonight."

He charged to a noble-looking elderly couple at another table, laughed with them, and snapped his fingers. John noticed Danielle staring at him. "Sir, did you see Danielle smile at me?"

"No, Hamilton," John said, recalling Megan's words: 'You make the same promises every year.' "Tonight, I wished I was sitting at our dining table, eating her New Years dinner."

Marcello, brought over several more bottles of Rossini wine and winked at an attractive brunette at the next table, and said "Excuse me." Hamilton poured himself another glass of red wine, and John said "Hamilton, eat some pagnotta, and drink slowly; we have to be at the base at 0500."

"Sir, that's eleven hours from now."

"Eleven hours is an eternity when your heart is someplace else."

Immediately, Lucian appeared with two pencil-thin waiters. He gleamed. "Each delicacy is grown at our countryside farm. Tonight, you are family." John leaned back. Hamilton sat upright and tied his napkin around his neck. The headwaiter announced, "We start first with: grilled tomato tarragon soup with croutons; herb-roasted whole brazino with potatoes, tomatoes, and olives; garlic-rubbed toast with fresh tomatoes and basil; and spaghetti with eggs, cured pork, and cheese."

And when later, Marcello and team captivated their stomach with perfection and pleasure of grilled lamb chops with asparagus dipped in creamed cheese sauce; veal scallops with prosciutto and sage; baked whole fish with slices of potatoes, Hamilton smiled. "Sir, I have never in my life tasted food like this."

"I can't eat anymore." John pushed his plate aside, and as if Lucian challenged him to a duel, Marcello presented desserts for the table: rich chocolate cake, cherry-lime cheesecake, tiramisu, deep dark chocolate cookies, dark chocolate-dipped cherry ice cream, and lime, orange, vanilla gelato.

"This is the best dessert I have ever had in my life." Hamilton grinned wider.

Danielle carried an assortment of cheeses and in the middle was Montasio. "That's the same cheese," John reflected.

In two snapped fingers, Marcello marched behind Lucian. "Captain, do enjoyed our cheese, it is from the mountains, near the Austrian border. It's found in the finest restaurants." As John enjoyed the raspberry liqueur, espresso was not far away. Hamilton savored the desserts.

By late evening, Marcello handed John the bill; Lucian received many one hundred American dollar bills. They shook hands, and smiled like old friends. "Grazie, Captain. My brother was mistaken, Captain, you are very much a gentleman. On your next visit to Rome, I hope you will bring your family." Hamilton slugged behind John.

Danielle nodded to John. "We hope you visit with us again." Hamilton's hands held his stomach. "Ciao," Danielle said.

In the taxi, John was silent. "Sir, I think I am ill." Hamilton exclaimed. The driver dropped them at Hotel Cesaré.

"Can you make it to your room Hamilton?"

"Yes, sir," he mumbled.

"Meet me in the lobby at 0400:30, and drink plenty of water tonight." We'll have coffee in the morning before we go to the base."

John watched the hotel manager assist Hamilton to the elevator. "Please take me to Café Rosa."

15

With the moonlight in the dark sky, the restaurant appeared closed. He could not tell if she was there; lights were out. He turned to leave and saw a small candle lit. He walked in. She was sitting on a white bench, smoking a MS Slim cigarette. A carafe of Cesanese on the floor, her eyes wondered to the bar counter glaring at a ceramic bowl full with fruits and vegetables. He sat in a chair facing her.

"We are closed," her rosy lips said.

"I'd like to have strong coffee, please?"

"I'm sorry, but strong coffee is not available tonight."

"What about a cold glass of water?" She put out her cigarette, walked behind the bar, returned with a wine glass in her hand. Her olive-green wrapped dress showed her slim waistline and stiff nipples.

She crossed her legs. "Why are you here? I waited for you for lunch and dinner, and now you are here?"

"I wanted to say goodbye. I'm flying out to the United States at four o'clock."

"Where did you eat dinner?" She lit a cigarette.

"We were instructed to go to Café Lucian."

"That monstrous place? Why would you eat there, when I can cook you a real Italian meal?"

"I said we were instructed—I cannot disobey an order."

"Do you do everything you are ordered to do?" Her adroit hand poured him a glass of wine. He kissed her sultry fingers, drank her wine, and she invited his lips. Neither could wait, except she did. She strode toward the hanging chandelier. "Will you do what I ask you?"

"Yes," he came to her.

She untied her dress, she reached out her hand. "*Non posso lasciarti*," she said.

"I don't know what that means."

"I cannot leave you," she said softly.

He drew her to him, holding her firmly.

"I am in love with you," she whispered.

He gently pushed her away. "How could that be?"

Her unbreakable hook pulled his arms back to where they belonged. "It takes a day for some people—it took me a moment." She kissed him; his hands stayed still. "Give me something." He could see their reflection in the shadow of the night. She whispered, "More, please," and more he did.

That early morning, John arrived at the hotel, scuttled in the shower. Within fifteen minutes, he was dressed and at the concierge's desk at four-fifteen. He settled Hamilton's and his account and relaxed on the cushy velvet sofa. As he jotted some notes, the manger handed him coffee. "Mr., Smith, we will miss you— your friend, not so much." John heard Hamilton's boots charging down the stairs. "Another cup for my friend," he said.

Hamilton walked to the desk; the concierge ignored him. "Hamilton your bill is paid. Come and have a seat for a few minutes before we leave."

"Captain Smith, for the first time, I understand why you stay at this hotel. Where else could you be guaranteed a cold shower and comfort in knowing you will make it to the base on time? As soon as I stepped in that shower, I remembered I was going home." The manager brought two more coffees.

"Hamilton, drink your coffee. It looks like snow flurries are escorting us back to the states."

"We left Georgia in the rain, returning in the snow. What kind of luck is that?"

Glaring at his watch, "its 0400:30 a.m.; drink up. Our Jet is the same; who cares about the damned snow?"

They entered the Rome Ciampino Airport Base and quickened their pace. Rossini's assistant saluted them and opened the door. Rapidly, Victorio closed the door avoiding his superior's cold-hearted eyes. A restless Colonel Rossini was spinning in his seat. "Gentlemen, my brother did not persuade you to stay in Rome?" He said cheerfully.

A frigid smile was pasted on John's face, "Thank you, sir. We will never forget Café Lucian."

"I will never forget the desserts and Danielle, sir," Hamilton said.

Rossini chuckled. "Yes, my niece is a treasured white rose—too bad she is to be married next month. Let's get to business—Captain, please have a seat. Lieutenant Hamilton, please excuse us for a brief moment. Captain, I want to say what a pleasure it has been to meet you and your lieutenant."

"Thank you, sir," John said.

Rossini opened a black leather brief case, handed the XLI canister to John. He inspected the canister.

"Captain, the packaged is secured," he muttered. "Please sign the authorization papers, then you can depart. Four eyes, one enemy—John signed straightaway. After a reserved silence, "The manifest is in order for your departure at 0600. My assistant is holding the telephone. Colonel Saddleback is on the line."

"Good morning, Colonel Saddleback," said Rossini. "Your men are here." He pressed the speaker line.

"Captain Smith, I'm told your companions are snow and sleet. Colonel Rossini informed me you are ready to return our cargo back to the United States. We were fortunate Colonel Rossini agreed to postpone his retirement to secure our cargo. Rossini and I are flying-fish friends. I always tell my men to stay focused and bring our girl back to where she belongs." He cleared his throat. "Colonel, would you give me a moment with my captain."

"Yes, of course." Rossini shut the door and faced John's dark eyes behind his glass-walled office.

Saddleback continued. "Captain Smith, I have some news about your family." John body was in control, but his heart was flying faster than a speeding bullet. He turned his back to Rossini. Colonel Saddleback coughed for a couple of moments. "Excuse me, Captain. Mrs. Smith telephoned New Year's Eve and said there was an emergency. She needed to speak to you right away. I informed her I would make sure you received the message. Your son was taken to the emergency room with a high fever, and he was in critical care for twenty four hours.

"Mrs. Smith telephoned yesterday, and she said the doctors allowed her to bring him home. He miraculously is cured. Mrs. Smith asked when you would be returning, and I told her today. She was happy, and wanted to assure you John Jr. is fine. Let's hope your son is completely recovered and the weather does not provide any longer delays. How old is your son, Captain?"

"He is seventeen years old and attending college this year, sir."

"You are a fortunate man to have a family. I am only conveying this message so that your journey back is completely removed from the distractions of yesterday." John rotated his head to Rossini, and reverses it back to the telephone.

"Colonel, I appreciate your concern. Mrs. Smith and I are proud of our son. I know how distressed she must have been to telephone, sir."

"No problem, Captain, come back with our jet, our cargo, and your family will see you tonight."

"Thank you, sir," he said eagerly. A soldier's shoulders were at ease, a fighter pilot ready for his mission; a new target within reach.

A radiant Rossini entered. "It's time for your departure, Captain. He extended his hand to John, who gripped his hand, and stared into Rossini's vain eyes.

"We are ready to leave, sir." John said emphatically.

Rossini withdrew his hand; he took a step back, and removed his eyeglasses. They slipped out of his fingers. As he bent down, John replayed his controlled colloquy with Saddleback.

"I wish you a safe journey, Captain," Rossini said, his black rimmed eyeglasses transfixed on John.

"Thank you, sir." He saluted and waited.

"That's all captain," Rossini said dryly.

"Yes, sir." John swiftly stepped out of his office.

"Ciao," Rossini said icily, opening his desk drawer, searching for his eye-drops.

Roundabout noon, Colonel Rossini scurried out of his office. "Vittorio, I have a conference call with Admiral J.K. Nuccio at 1400; make sure my driver is ready downstairs. Call my wife and tell her we are entertaining my brother Lucian and Miriam for dinner tonight."

A black four-door Mercedes droved steadily in bustling traffic; Rossini tapped his watch. "Take the short-cut to Café Rosa." He had two cups of espresso and wanted a third. "Pronto," the driver said. The closed signed was in the window. The driver opened Rossin's door. "I won't need you the rest of the day."

Two tables were turned over outside, hasty hands grasped the brass knob, heartburn ignited a shout. "Natalie, where the hell are you?" He yelled, taking off his coat.

"I'll be right out," she mumbled.

His hands were on his hips, and he looked at the hanging chandelier that was loose. "Natalie," he bellowed.

"What do you want?" She was barefoot; her green dress looked slept in. A duty-free Marlboro cigarette was in her hand. She sat at the bar stool smoking, wiping the last tears from her dry mascara eyes.

He lit his own cigarette and stood close to her waist. "I thought you would want to know your lover is gone. I made sure he left today. He departed our dear Rome exactly at five forty-five this morning."

"He was not my lover; you are my lover, he was my love." He stroked her sweaty hair. She hopped out her chair, staggered to the front door, and turned the closed sign to open.

"Why would you close the café at the busiest time of the day, we could lose money."

She slogged behind the bar, turned on the juke box, and the phonograph played, "Madame Butterfly." Tears returned. Her eyes were pink, both palms wiped her face. A hard fist thumped the bar, swift feet jump off his seat.

"Turn down that music," he pouted, "I don't have time. I must be back in an hour."

"I don't want to be with you anymore, this is what I am telling you."

He raced behind the bar, and switched off the juke box. "Come here," he demanded.

"No," she screamed.

"You can work at Café Lucian." Perspiration dripped down his Tuscany-tanned skin. She stared at the heavy black dye on his eyebrows. He kissed her pale lips and neck. "Should we keep Café Rosa opened or closed?"

"Opened," she said and moved quickly away.

He grinned, glided his oversized boots to the door, and turned the sign back to closed. His fat, fastidious hand unbuttoned his shirt. Natalie glared at his portly waist.

The disappointment in her lovely eyes hated him. "Captain Smith will be making love to his wife tonight. Do you think I would share you with another man?"

The perfectly starched shirt was folded with gentle care; he placed it beside the ceramic bowl on the circular, paneled oak bar. Her toned arms swept the floor in a rapid pace; Natalie pretended she was in another place.

His concentrated eyes pierced at the broom. "What do you wish?" He could taste her. And his colonel's hand pointed to the spotless floor.

The black and white tile was cold; her body lay alongside empty wine bottles. He removed his economical eyeglasses, handed them to her. Her left

W. D. Moore

hand loosely held his bifocals, the right hand firmly held her gold-plated, Vatican cross necklace.

"Unlock your legs, Natalie; I have to punish you for being bad. Do you want me to punish you?" She did not answer. He slapped her face.

"Yes," she said.

"Yes, what?" he asked? She closed her eyes. "Yes, please."

Her swollen eyes felt severe pain, far worse than years before. He was grunting, glowing; she hoped she was dead. He gouged at her neck, ripped away her necklace. "He's trying to kill me," she thought. Rossini's satisfied shut eyes did not witness her spellbound eyes look at the wine bottles on her right. Hot sticky sweat touched her face, as she attempted to move away.

"You stay or I will hurt you all day," he shouted.

The power of strong-minded hand managed to grasp onto an empty bottle. She hit him hard on his head, rolled his robust stomach off her body. She was taller than he. She grabbed another bottle marked "Rossin's Vintage" and hit him harder. Café Rosa is mine," her voice screamed. She snatched his white shirt off the solid bar, and she tossed it on Rossini's dead-eyed face.

Liberty and a newborn life energized her firefly feet running to her apartment. Without glancing at herself in the bathroom mirror, she reached in the rust urn, grabbed a wooden box, and poured three teaspoons of Tuscan herbs in the tub water to heal her body.

After one hour passed, she maneuvered her soul out of her cast-iron tub. Her body stood in the front of the marble-basin, pedestal sink. She gently caressed her bruised neck. There was a red rose in a silver chalice that Rossini had given her two days ago. Her sturdy hands demolished it in shreds, casting the petal in the Flushometer toilet.

In her bedroom, she picked up her lime blanket and wrapped it around her body. Her heart was in the past, thinking of John's tender touch. Pillows, linen, and his smell endured in her bed. She held onto each morsel of rapture until the telephone rang. Her mind returned to the present. The rings stopped. Natalie lit a thin MS cigarette and dialed his number. "Papa, I need your help."

Traffic, tourists, and taxis were reminding her of her uncle's body down stairs. She closed the leaded stained-glass window. "Sleep is what I need." She awoke eighty minutes later and slipped into a burgundy kimono silk robe. "If I didn't love Café Rosa I could leave Rome." In a quick moment, she heard the door open, and hurried downstairs.

Lucian and Marcello strolled in; they watched Natalie point her fingers to the bar. Her body shook, she leaned on the stairway banister. Her papa's old-fashioned eyes never left her.

"Marcello, clean up this mess, your sister has to open up the restaurant for dinner." Natalie's head faced her clear toes. Lucian smiled at his daughter, for he loved her more than any of his five children. His eyes scanned each inch of the restaurant. "It's done; I have 100 shares of the business." She proceeded to tread her feet to her apartment. He kissed his oldest daughter's unsteady hands. "I will sign over Café Rosa to you."

"Yes, papa," she said. Lucian patted her mother's nose, pinched her father's cheeks, and paused. "Natalie, Mama misses you; she wishes your presence for commensality on Sunday.

"Yes papa," she muttered. He released her steady hand. She was gone.

"Good," he said, glaring at Marcello struggling with his uncle's legs. He snapped his fingers. "Marcello, call your cousins to help you, or your football team. Natalie will have customers soon."

PART III

16

That afternoon in Atlanta, Georgia, on Chester Street, the winds of Megan's mind traced her steps from a Christmas night with Big Boy Blue to New Year's Eve with John Jr. at Crawford W. Long Hospital. He had a temperature as high as 105°F, chills, cough, and chest pains. She worried and feared the worst. He was in critical care for twenty-four hours. The resident physician tried to reassure her to have hope. "Let the medicine do its work," Dr. Peter Miller had said. She pleaded to stay him in his room, to be by his side.

"I am his mother," she screamed. The doctor remained firm, and said "no." She stayed in the emergency waiting room. Her mind in a whirlwind, "twenty-four hours is a death sentence." She looked out the window onto Peachtree Street; the traffic was bumper-to-bumper on the warmest day in January. "John Jr. could die; days will continue whether he is here or not."

She marched back to her son's room, Dr. Miller met her outside his door.

"Your son has pneumonia, please wait in emergency. Is there a family member who can be with you?" Megan sobbed violently in her heart. She staggered back to the waiting room and went to the busily sounds of life outside her heart. Hours later, she picked up the pay phone and requested to speak to Colonel Saddleback. "Mrs. Smith your husband cannot be reached at this time. I am sure your son will be fine. Please call me as soon as the doctor provides you with an updated condition of your son." She slammed the phone. She rolled up in a white, vinyl lounge chair, crossed her arms around her body, and closed her eyes to keep from going mad.

New Year's day, the dark earth had stopped. Dr. Miller came to Megan. "Mrs. Smith, your son is asking for you." Her calisthenics-toned legs leaped into his room, wiping away fresh, happy tears.

"Hey Mom." He looked like her healthy son. Dr. Miller's hands were on John Jr.'s forehead, facing his mother.

"Mrs. Smith, your son is a strong young man—it must be from his parents. He told me your husband is a fighter pilot in the Air Force. It is a miracle he has recovered in less than twenty-four hours. His chart gives me no reason to keep him here. I'm checking him out; I know you will take better care of him at home. Make sure he rests for forty-eight hours and takes his medicine. He can have soup, liquids, and plenty of water for a few days."

Within an hour, John Jr. was asleep in his bed. Megan telephoned Colonel Saddleback with the good news and slogged to the kitchen.

"How many thousands of hours, months, and years have I had to take care of John Jr. alone? Injuries from little league, junior league, baseball, and basketball practice, Chicken pox, and colds, while my husband is on a classified assignment. And every time, I think I can't handle it, a miracle happens."

She reached for her large, black kettle pot, the only possession she cherished from her mother's house, preparing her momma's chicken soup: whole chicken, onions, carrots, potatoes, garlic, and peppers. She added spices and her secret ingredient from Miss May Perry.

The soup was on the stove, she undressed, went into the bathroom. She gently dry-brushed her skin, starting, with her winsome hands to her poppy-colored feet. She turned on the shower, soothing her soul with the sweet lavender soap.

"My passion for Blue almost became more important than the love of our family. What if he did not leave? What if John Jr. saw him in my bed? And what if John came home unexpectedly?"

Torrential tears were the companion of steaming water. "God, I promise, no more Blue." She slipped in black bell-bottom pants, white knitted sweater and stared at her over-flowing wet waves and dry face. The telephone rang. "Oh John, is it you?"

"Mrs. Smith, Captain Smith, he will be home tonight," Captain Saddleback said.

"Thank you, for calling," she said warmly.

"Not at all; I'm happy to know your son is doing well."

She peeked in on John Jr.—he was snoring. She placed another blanket over him, and tried to sit quietly in his 'Atlanta Braves Bean Bag' chair. All of a sudden, she heard. "Mommy, is that chicken soup, I smell?"

Megan hopped out of the chair and kissed his forehead. "You haven't called me that name since you were a child, and yes, I'm cooking soup. Go back to sleep and when it is ready; I will bring you a bowl. Your dad is on his way home."

"Mom, is Dad really coming home?"

"Yes, sweetheart, he is on his way home." She closed her eyes, wrapped her body like a baby and prayed: "God, forgive me for being stupid; please help me to keep away from Blue." She was in a deep sleep for ten minutes. Her heart awoke in fear. "Is he here?" She bolted to her bedroom, looked, and stopped. "I was dreaming." Returning to John Jr.'s room, she tried to make a bed in the red and blue bean bag. With her hands as her pillow, she fell asleep.

Black overcast blue, no clouds smoking through, the smooth warm night— John's "Pony Car" skirted in the drive way at ten o'clock. Quickly, he grabbed his one bag, entered his home. He smelled the chicken soup at the door; the lights were out, except in the kitchen. He removed his sparkling boots, hurried upstairs, and dropped his coat on the banister.

"My family," he muttered. His son was sleeping in his bed; his wife was sleeping in his son's favorite chair. Her loose hair over her shoulders covering half her breathtaking face. Her lingering legs hung on to her new bed. "She is ravishing—the reason I have a family," he thought.

He carried her to their bed. She awakened, "John, you're home." He kissed her Dorothy Dandridge lips; she dozed back to sleep. He tiptoed to John Jr.'s room.

"Dad, you're home," John Jr. yawned.

"How do you feel, Son?" "Oh, I'm better, but Mom won't believe me. She has been sleeping in my room." John's fatherly hands felt his son's forehead, pulled the covers to his neck.

"Do you need anything, Son?"

"I'm much better; the doctor said I have to stay in bed for another day, and then I can move around."

"I'm sorry I was not home to help take care of you, John Jr."

"Dad, you know Mom takes care, and she gave Dr. Miller a hard time. She knows more than the doctor. He said, "She should have been a doctor."

"Son, go back to sleep. In the morning, I'm cooking breakfast."

"I can't wait; can we have blueberry pancakes, sausages, eggs too?"

"We'll ask your mom the approved menu. I love you; go back to sleep."

"OK, Dad."

Quietly, he removed his shirt and pants, and laid himself behind her warm body. He caressed her smooth skin, her rain forest hair, and his head landed home on her breast. "Thank you for putting me to bed. I forgot how good it feels to lie down." Her eyes were bright and wide; he kissed her baby lips. "I'm glad you are home." John held her through the early morning sunrise, body to body in each other's eyes.

At dawn, John heard Megan's love birds singing. She was sleeping soundly. He moved slowly to check up on John Jr. He stood watching his son for a longtime, yawned and return to bed. He rested his head on her firm stomach. She awoke and rubbed his smooth head. "How is he?" she asked.

"Your son is dreaming about pancakes. What did you give him yesterday?"

"I gave him lots of love and plenty of chicken soup."

"That's your secret weapon, Baby. John Jr. said the doctor thinks you should have become a physician."

"Dr. Peter Miller telephoned to see how he was doing; later he asked the ingredients in my chicken soup."

He undressed her. Her arms stretched high. "Are you sick, Baby? Let's never argue again before you leave on an assignment."

He took a moment and swiftly held her face. "I was afraid I was losing you."

Her eyes were misty. "I love you." He kissed her lips on the yellow butterfly pillow, his hands touched her bikini waxed body. He was strong.

"My God," she said to herself. "He's skillful, my man, my husband— it's like our honeymoon night, when I became his woman."

Both pilot hands pushed back her wavy hair. "Baby," he said. "Hold on."

17

Six months passed, it was June 15, 1973. "Baby, I'll be back before dinner. Can we eat at seven o'clock tonight?" John asked, dashing to his automobile.

"John, you're not flying out today are you? Your son's party is tomorrow."

"No, I told you, it's only a meeting. See you by seven this evening." In reverse, he drove his red Mustang from their driveway like a fiery jet on Chester Street to Dobbins Air Base.

With afternoon laundry to do, Megan stopped in John Jr.'s room, a large basket in hand. The telephone rang.

"Hello," Megan said briskly.

"Hi darling, what time is the party," Miss May Perry said jubilantly.

"Hi, Aunt May; it's tomorrow at five o'clock, but you can come early." She placed the basket on the floor. "This will take a while," she thought.

The ROTC Counselor at Eden High was waiting for his three-thirty appointment with John Jr.; who was rushing to Sergeant Holley Street—then he walked at a slow pace when he thought about his Mom. "I feel Dad wants me to pursue a career in the military, I know Mom wants me at Morehouse. I've been Mom's best friend while Dad's been away, and Dad's my best friend when he's home. Even if he misses my football games, when he's home, he's engrossed in every detail. My parents are my friends; I just want to be like my Dad.

"I wanted to join the ROTC in the eighth grade, and changed my mind, because Mom would have had a heart attack. I'm going my own way. This time, I am not changing my mind." He knocked on the door.

"Yes," Sergeant Holley Street said politely.

"Can I come in, sir?" John Jr. asked.

"Son, I've been waiting for you; I received word from the admissions office months ago that you got accepted at West Point in New York. Congratulations. Why did you wait until the last day of school to stop by? It was never a doubt they would accept you with your grades. Of course, it helped that your father is a captain in the Air Force. I confirmed your character at Eden; the teachers' comments on your ability to listen—believe me—this is the real reason you got in."

"Thank you, Sir," John Jr. grinned.

"Don't thank me. Keep in touch—let me know how you are doing. I will be available to speak to you anytime on the telephone. Things were different when I joined the service twenty-six years ago. I went to Tuskegee, but I didn't make the cut in the fighter pilot training program. Shoot, I didn't care; I was interested in being a soldier. Back then, any kind of solider would have made me happy. Sit down son, how does it feel, your last day in high school?"

Chatter continued for two more hours. When John Jr. managed to leave, he started walking home. "Today is Friday; by July, I will be at West Point Military Academy. I can't wait." He took a deep breath. "What about Mom? She is planning a big party tomorrow to celebrate my graduation from high school. Dad is going to kill me. I promised him I would tell her about West Point. I never did. I'll tell her when I get home."

He stared at the grey-blue overcast clouds. "For once, I wish there was a tornado watch and Mom would have to cancel the party. I heard some guys are leaving this Sunday to tour New York City and then head straight to West Point on Tuesday. I wish I could go." He paused, "I have to think about Mom."

Skipping along, he said, "And Blue, the coach brags to everyone that he got accepted at the Ohio State University. Who cares?"

"Anyway, Dad's been home. He said he was retiring this year. If he does, Mom won't be sad about me leaving."

The orange 1972 Chevrolet Vega hatchback passed John Jr. Sergeant Holley Street saw the young man he wanted to be. He blew his horn at him and waved. He drove leisurely. WAOK radio played a commercial; he ignored the advertisement for Afro Sheen. "He's lucky he got a father with connections that can make a telephone call. Shoot, maybe I could have been him, but not really. That was never my concern; I wanted anything in red. I danced with a girl. She asked, "What song is that were dancing to?" I said, "It don't matter, Baby, just dance." I spent two nights in jail in 1947. I was nineteen and found out later, the girl was fifteen. It convinced me, girls in red with sexy legs were dangerous. I hitched a ride from Georgia to Mobile; somehow, I landed at the footsteps of Tuskegee, Alabama." He speeded his GM Vega, and instantly stopped at the yellow traffic light. He smiled, stared, and watched three ponytail teenagers in miniskirts swish by.

Carrying his book bag, John Jr. strolled into the house. His dad's car was gone, his mom's car was parked an inch on the grass. "Mom," he said audibly. "Maybe she went out with Dad." He opened the refrigerator, grabbed two Coca-Cola bottles and jogged to his room. He tossed his books and picked up the phone. "Hey Willie," he said, plunging into his bean bag.

In the basement, Megan was having a conversation with the "Speed Queen" set. "Please don't break down today, I have so much work to do. It's clanking in response," she laughed. She was sweating, fanning while listening to the rattling noise. A full load was in the dryer, she closed it and moments later, a hollering racket. "The dryer belt is broken, it must be."

John Jr. stomped to the basement. "Mom, who were you talking to?" She opened the dryer door, the clothes were damp.

"You're undershirts, school shirts, and favorite Atlanta Braves' tee shirts are in the dryer. I have a party to plan. Can you hang you're the clothes on the line, or wait until your father buys a new dryer?"

She stormed past him. "I'm going to take a bath before I start dinner." She shrilled and decided to take a shower.

Bright and early Saturday morning Megan was grocery shopping at Kroger's. She peeked in the Cashin Coach bag. "Where is my list? Oh, good, I knew I was forgetting something. I always do, and then I have to rush back to the store."

She bought: baking soda, vanilla soda, drinking soda for the house. In the bread section, she heard, "Hello Megan, I see you are shopping today also."

"Vinnie, how are you feeling today?" Megan kissed her rosy cheeks.

"I'm fine, even though my left knee is hurting, but I have to make an effort for my nephew, Blue. He'll be going to a university in Ohio; his parents cannot make it to his graduation. I thought somebody should care."

"I'm sure your nephew will appreciate whatever you do for him. I do have to run; I am having a big party for my son today." Megan hurried to the cash register.

"Home at last," she thought, a quarter of an hour later. Groceries on the country table, baking pans on the fine wood countertop, her mind would leave her a bit. "I can't think of Big Boy Blue right now. I must concentrate on John Jr.'s special day. My son, my baby is going to college."

The next few moments, she listened to the chirping noise of birds on the windowsill. Easing into her plastic gloves, she started washing dishes; she watched the family of birds. "I remember when John Jr. weighed six pounds.

We stepped into the house; he started crying and would not stop. He was wrapped in an ivory cashmere throw—from John's mother, Ella. I couldn't take off my coat. I was afraid to let him out of my arms.

"Holding him, rocking him; he still wouldn't stop crying. I paced the red oak floor singing, Jesus loves you, yes I know, Jesus loves you, Oh, yes I know; Oh, yes he does, and Mommy, Daddy, Grandma, and Grandpa, too. I circled him around for hours until he fell asleep. John would hold him at first, he was fearful of squashing our small son with his large hands." After a few teardrops, "Megan, don't cry now; you have too much work to do." She grabbed the large serrated knife, chopped two pounds of Swiss dark chocolate for John Jr.'s celebration cake.

By four in the afternoon, guests arrived, and Megan was undisturbed. She prepared the home-cooked feast, arranged flowers, and entertained everyone. Roundabout fifty people in the Smith's household: relatives from Virginia, across Georgia, and California. Megan was the Southern belle of the ball, everyone talked about her beauty and poise. John kept his proud eyes on John Jr.; his pleased eyes on his wife.

It was John Jr.'s job to be responsible for the music; her husband was responsible for mixing cocktails, and both were responsible for keeping Miss May Perry at bay.

Somehow, there was space for their guests to move throughout the living room, dining room, and family room, but not the kitchen. Only husband and son were allowed entrance.

On the block table were desserts: carrot cake, pound cake, white cake, and gingerbread. In the center of the kitchen, the farmhouse table paraded sweet potato pies, apple pies, peach cobbler pies, chocolate chip cookies, and two double dark chocolate cakes.

Since Sauvignon Blancs and dry rosé wine were plenty, John took a break from the special cocktails bar. Long Island Ice tea in his hand, he stood by the rear window. John Jr. was drinking sweet ice tea. In a low tone, he said, "Dad, thanks for your help at West Point."

"I'm delighted about your determination to follow your heart. Look at your mother, how beautiful she looks. She glows whenever your name is mentioned. I'm a bit dismayed—only you and I know your true intentions. Your mom is unaware; she can recite every famous person who attended Morehouse. We talked about this, son. By the time I came home last night from the base, your mom was asleep; she darted out early this morning. Under the pillows, I heard her on the telephone speaking to Uncle Charles about Morehouse. Your cousin Donald is attending and they were hoping you two could be roommates."

"Dad, I was going to tell Mom yesterday, but she was upset about the dryer, mad as heck, and I couldn't talk to her."

"You have had months, since Christmas, to tell her your intention, son. I left this job for you. If you are going to be a soldier, you will have to obey orders-whether you like them or not. I gave you an order, and you failed. I'm your father and will give you another chance. This will never happen at West Point Academy. Nothing I could say would make your superior officer give you a second opportunity. Are you certain you want a career in the military?"

"Yes, Dad," he said emphatically.

"As for a new washer and dryer, it's been purchased as a surprise to your mother after you depart for New York." He watched Miss May Perry and Megan hugged.

"You know your grandfather, Duke, never went to college. When he was seventeen years old, your great grandfather said, "You are a grown man now, and it's time that you leave my house. We don't have room for two men in my house. My father said, "I didn't have parents who read books to me; I was a below-average student and barely graduated from Kelly Miller high school in Clarksburg, West Virginia. I knew I couldn't go to college." He told me a story of when he was in the eighth grade, in his English class and Mrs. Porter, said it was his turn to read the next paragraph from The Cricket on the Hearth. He rose, and father was more afraid that moment than any beatings he got from my grandfather. Your grandfather started reading the first sentence. He couldn't finish it, because he mispronounced many of the words. The students giggled, he failed the class, and never opened his mouth again.

"Grandmother Ella was raised different; she was educated, graduated from my alma mater, West Virginia for Coloreds. Her family threatened to change their will when she married Dad. Grandmother's father was Greek; her mother was from Aswan, Egypt. But then, you know this story. The point is they constantly threatened to disown her. Mom received her inheritance, and it paid for my education. I received the same, and it will pay for yours.

"If mother was not healing from her hip operation, they would be here. Your Grandfather Duke takes care of her, refuses to leave his Ella's side. She writes about your grandfather, and he writes to me about her.

"The day I graduated from West Virginia State, he pretended he was not proud, but I saw pride in his eyes. He gave me a hard time throughout, but his sternness helped me survive my training at Mather Air Force Base. I tell you this, because you are soon to leave your home, your mother and I will never leave you."

Tears ran down John Jr.'s face. "Dad, I love you and Mom. Why don't we talk like this more?"

"I know, Son. When I'm home, I just want the rapture of my family's love, and I don't make the time." He stared at his father's loving eyes and at his mother. Megan observed their intense conversation. She wondered what they were talking about, and suddenly she stopped and looked at the kitchen screen door. She sensed Blue. Her heart was beating, praying it was not true.

Her son peered at her panicked eyes. "Dad, I'm going to see if there is any chocolate cake left." He walked toward his mother; Miss May Perry watched them. John started to follow John Jr. Miss May Perry approached him.

"John, I been waiting for you to bring me a drink. What kind of host are you?"

"Aunt May, I was on my way to sit with you." She grabbed John's arms leading him to the bar.

"John, I'll take vodka straight up." She grinned and her yellow gold diamond ring sparkled holding the crystal glass.

Family and friends were shaking John Jr.'s hand, patting him on the back, babies were crying, and Megan stared at Blue. Blue smiled. John Jr. secured her shoulder. "Mother," he whispered. "Big Boy Blue is not invited." Instantly he shut the door.

18

And when in the morning, John cooked pancakes, waffles, Canadian bacon. He laid a warm sauceboat of maple syrup, blueberries, and sweet butter on the table. John Jr. told his mom he was attending West Point Military Academy in New York. He rejected the scholarship at Morehouse College; he had to be on campus the following Tuesday, June 26th.

Megan stared in her husband's eyes. "He already knew," she thought. She glared at her son; "He lied to me," she cried inside her mind. She was speechless, solemn. She ceased eating, left the kitchen table.

She wallowed in the backyard. Later on, she sat underneath the willow tree, ponderous, in thought. She slipped off her green mule shoes, her red-painted toes wiggled in the grass.

A tiger swallowtail butterfly rested on her knee. "Where did you come from?" Suddenly, it flew away. She followed it far in the blue sky.

"Blue," she quietly echoed to herself. She closed her eyes. "I love you."

He spotted her from his Aunt Rose's sitting room. Their eyes met. They spoke the same language. She dusted herself off, dragged her heart back in the house.

A few days later; grey overcast blue, white clouds smoking through. Megan was changing the bed linen in her bedroom. The telephone rang.

"Baby, sit down, a minute," John said placidly.

"Why, what's wrong?" she asked curtly.

"That was Miss May Perry on the telephone; she received a telephone call about your father. Daddy Windom passed away."

"Oh, is that all? I thought you were sick or something." She stared serenely at him. "Look at these new satin sheets; I bought two colors: pink and blue at Neiman Marcus. Can you believe they were on sale? Baby, isn't the weather perfect for watching an old classic movie. Maybe we can find a Bette Davis movie, The Letter on the Turner channel later. "I'll make the popcorn while you stir the cocktails."

His transfixed eyes observed his wife's calm manner. And in a casual way she said, "I'll have to find something to wear. I know, I'll wear my yellow dress you like to the funeral."

The memorial service was Sunday, June 24th at Little Friend's Baptist Church on Friendship Street. Megan was baptized at seven years old. Her momma, Lina, taught Sunday school and was an usher every other Sunday. The church was a small, crisp, white colonial: two gigantic peach trees on five acres of grounds, parking space was the landscaped lawn, one hundred parishioners had ample room for Sunday's traditional family picnics.

As a child, Megan's white patent leather shoes skipped on the concrete steps. She smelled the fried chicken, collard greens, and hot rolls being prepared by the twelve-ladies fellowship committee in the basement.

Lina held Megan's white gloves while walking in church together. "Baby, every generation of the Muttons has been members of Little Friends Baptist Church." Megan's eyes rolled throughout the pews. In her Shirley-Temple curls, she hopped along, dressed in a yellow ribbon, yellow dress, and white socks to their usual seats.

"Momma, where is Daddy?"

Daddy Windom never stepped inside of a church. He didn't believe in God. Lina waved her Jesus Christ fan thinking about his words, "If I want to see God; all I need to do is to look at myself in the mirror." Lina stopped asking him to come, but she brought him church dinner. He ate it without delay.

This mournful morning, Megan wore: a yellow dress, a long black ribbon tied loosely around her ponytailed hair, black patent leather dress-heeled sandals, and white fishnet gloves. The church choir sang: "This Little Light of Mine, I'm Gonne Let it Shine." The Reverend Friendship rose, spoke in a somber tone, "Friends, we are here to send off our sister's husband, Mitchell Windom Mutton, to heaven. Lina's daughter, Megan is here with her family, and we welcome them with love this sad Sunday. Mrs. Smith, please come up and express your warmhearted words."

Her billowy bright dress flowed in a slow motion to the podium. She stared in her husband's eyes, cleared her throat before saying, "Reverend Friendship, friends, my momma, Lina, loved this church. Every generation of my momma's family loved this church. I grew up loving our church. I'm sorry to say, my daddy didn't believe in church, but he loved chicken dinners from Little Friends Baptist Church.

"Daddy Windom was a handsome man, hard man, maybe it is why my momma was soft. She wanted me to know the difference. She would say to my daddy, "One day, you gonna look in the mirror, and see the devil." He paid her no mind. He went out drinking with his friends on Saturday nights. Three days ago, he died from liver disease. His light skin, straight hair, wanton smile brought women to their feet. Daddy Windom decided he didn't want to be married to my mommy anymore.

"My momma passed two years after I married. Daddy Windom was busy drinking moonshine some place. He could not make it to her funeral. Still, I know my momma loved him. In the end, they will be joined together where Momma wanted them to be, right here at Little Friends Baptist Church."

The congregation applauded, the six-man choir sang "I Got a Feeling Everything Gonna Be Alright." Megan's self-satisfied grace jetted back to her seat. John held her left hand, John Jr. held her right. In a split second, she tapped her fluid fingers on their knuckles, as if she was playing Mozart's piano Concerto No. 21. John Jr. smirked, John did not. She was humming; her head was on John's shoulders. She whispered in his ear, "Baby, make sure we get three dinners to go, before we bury him."

She closed her unforgiving eyes, counting the minutes, when they could leave Little Friends Baptist church.

19

It was a family barbecue the next day. John Jr. was scheduled to depart on Delta flight 287 at six o'clock Tuesday morning to New York. Five other cadets and he would be at Kennedy Airport to meet Sergeant Hindsbrook, who was transporting them to West Point, New York. "There is no reason to wait for the Fourth of July to barbecue; it's only the three of us," her tense voice said, laying potato salad, buttered rolls on the glass patio table.

They stretched the night, talking, laughing, father and son. She listened and saw a strong connection between them. "It's like they are brothers," she said silently to herself.

At midnight, the men were sitting at the kitchen table eating butter-pecan ice cream, and Oreo cookies. She kissed John Jr. "I know your dad is dropping you off to the airport at four-thirty in the morning; I won't be going with you. I love you, and I am proud of you, Son."

He hugged Megan. "Mom, I'll be home for Christmas; that's only six months away." His eyes choked up. "I love you Mom."

"I love you more." She left them standing; they watched her move slowly to the staircase.

The lights were out an hour later. When John came to bed, Megan was asleep. He laid close to her, placid in peace.

She awoke from the door being shut. She jumped out of bed, watched John Jr. being driven away. Sitting at her vanity, she recognized her mother's eyes, when her husband broke her heart. She went back to bed. Dreaming of water, she floated in a canoe, drowned in the sea. "I have no more tears left," she bellowed.

Wednesday, July 4th; the weather was a beautiful kind of day. They had a romantic dinner in the dining room. An aged terra cotta hurricane was the centerpiece, surrounded by red roses from John. She prepared oven-baked barbecue ribs, baked beans, burnt macaroni and cheese. "A first time," she said. He ate every bit of it, pleading for seconds, anything to please her.

Late at night, John was lying in bed waiting for her. She cleaned the kitchen, the dishes sparkled, and leftovers were wrapped and sealed in the ice box. She had no excuse to stay downstairs.

If she thought of how both her husband and son deceived her, she wanted to hate them. And she did. She would take turns hating John one day, John Jr. the next day, and every other day hated them both.

"Baby, come to bed, what are you doing?" John said anxiously, from the staircase.

"I'll be up in a few minutes," she snapped. Megan removed her sky-blue apron and yearned for Big Boy Blue. "He wants me too, I want him." She turned the kitchen light out, checked the front door, and continued to speak her mind. "John never remembers to lock the door. He doesn't think any man could break in and harm his family. In our marriage, he has been home temporarily. It's been me raising our son; it was I who breast-fed him, I who trained him on his first bicycle."

He charged down the staircase; she rearranged the Laurel Green velvet pillows on the sofa. His black silk pajama pants still had the tag dangling. "I forgot to take it off. Oh, so what? I don't care," she sighed.

"Baby, what's wrong? John Jr. is fine; he likes West Point."

She flipped her pink fluffy slippers at his bare feet. "John, I don't understand why John Jr. did not tell me he was not attending Morehouse College. Especially, since he received a full scholarship. All this time, he gave me, our family, the impression he wanted to go there. We talked about it often through the years when you were away. I had no idea he contemplated military school."

She thrust one pillow on the arm chair and flopped into the love sofa; she crossed her arms and legs. He smiled at the fitted safari-print dress that rose high, gazing at her voluptuous bosom. "I want to make love; she wants to fight," he said to himself. "And yet," he said. "Our son is not a boy anymore. He is a man. John Jr. told me he tried to tell you, and every time, he was afraid to break his mother's heart. I ordered him to speak to you; he promised me he would."

"But, John, while you have been on missions, I have been here morning, noon, and night. I don't understand why he could not talk to me."

He was quiet and flopped on the floor beside her ankles. He stroked her feet, massaged her smooth legs, and rubbed her firm thighs. She pushed his hands away. "John, can we finish this conversation?"

He settled himself on the sofa and sternly said, "John Jr. is my son; if I am flying one-hundred-thousand miles from home, my son is our son, my wife is my wife. My home is our home. My family is our family. The day before his celebration party, our son came to tell you he had changed his mind. He said you were angry about the dryer and rushed to take a bath."

"What did he think?" her mind spinning in sheer horror. "Did John Jr. suspect my relationship with Blue? Is this the real reason he left home? Oh, my God, does he know?" Four tears of fear rolled down her flustered face.

The strength and stability of John's arms held her head close to his heart. "Baby, I'm here, I'm not leaving you; you won't be alone, and I love you." He gently wiped away her weepy eyes. She kissed his potent lips. They held each other's bodies tight. "Baby," John said, "You been working too hard, let your man take care of you tonight."

She instead took extra care of her husband. They made love on the love sofa; he carried her to their bed where he loved her again.

Days changed but Megan's heart remained unchanged. Her subconscious mind said, "How could my husband and son conspire against me?"

Sometimes, she barely looked at John. Whenever, John Jr. telephoned, she made an excuse not to speak to him.

At Blue's house, he was a caged animal in heat for Megan. He saw her with her husband, never alone. He felt her heart; once their eyes met, nothing more. It rained every day. "Everything is against me, except you, Baby. I know you love me." He stretched on his "flat bench press," determined to perform 600 sit ups. He stopped at 500. "Damn," he said, dialing her number.

"Hey Savannah, it's Blue, you still don't like me? I've been thinking about you. Can I come over?"

Still, the day came, Blue Bedford had to leave for college on July 9. He heard her voice ringing in his head. He grabbed his red Buckeye's duffle bag, left a note for his Aunt Rose, "Auntie, your car will be at the lower level parking lot garage. Don't forget to bring your set of keys; otherwise, you have to come to Ohio to get mine. I'll call you sometime, Blue." Megan's house was quiet. "Sleeping late," Blue said. "Too bad his damn airplane doesn't explode on the Hartsfield runway."

Driving fast on I-75, he made a U-turn, and drove to downtown, to Piedmont Park. He left the keys in the car, and slammed the door. He sprinted faster than an eagle until his heart forced him to stop. "What time is it? It's eight o'clock; I got two hours to make my flight."

Blue rung the door bell, she had pink rollers in her hair. "Big Boy Blue," what are you doing here? My parents just drove off to work." He put his left foot in the door, charged in. "Hello Savannah, I'm coming in." Her Vaseline lips let him kiss her, her Clark University tee shirt covered her behind. "Blue, wait a minute," he pushed her in the brown crush chair; he unzipped himself; she let him in. A short time later, he zipped himself right up. "Blue, why so fast, hard?"

"Why you let me in, if you didn't want it? I gave it to you like I always do." His raw hand reached for the door knob.

Savannah started taking the rollers out of her hair. "You leaving?" She rushed to get the last roller out.

"Yea, I got a plane to catch."

"But, you just got here, Blue. Don't go, let's talk a bit."

He stared at her disheveled hair. "I don't have time."

She brushed her hair off her face, removed her tee shirt, nuzzled in closer to his lips. He released his hand from the door. She sensed a changed desire. "I got him," she cheered inside her mind. She unzipped his jeans, they loved each other longer. Savannah's head was on his chest; she was giddy. "Blue, I love you."

His eyes were tight. "Megan," he whispered.

"Megan," she yelled. "Who is Megan?" Her tears falling, her mouth screaming in pain. "How could you call me another girl's name?"

He stared at her full waist. "Savannah, looks like you put on some weight." His rocklike hand grasped the door.

"You treat me like a nobody," she hollered. "Are you a nobody too?"

He dashed to the Nova. In ten minutes, he turned into Delta Terminal. The sky shone a fluorescent blue. "Megan," he said. "Keep looking at the sky, Baby; we'll be together. I love you, and I'll be back."

The eighth month of the year, August, was humid, home life was becoming an obstacle course for John. He was an officer at the base; at home, studying the movements of Megan, he watched her in the yard, humming with the love birds, hearing her laughter daily with Miss May Perry.

On Labor Day, after a late lunch, John turned on a basketball play-off game, between the Los Angeles-Lakers and the New York Knicks. He lounged on the checkered sofa in the family room. At the end of the first quarter,

Megan hopped on his lap and watched the game with him; she cuddled, he caressed, they ate her homemade oatmeal cookies.

At half-time, she whispered in his ear, "I love you John; your beauty is all I see."

"And I love you, my darling, all of you," he said, kissing her passionately. By the end of the third-quarter, she made her quick and easy curry-flavored fettuccine. And then in the middle of the fourth-quarter; he turned off the television, used his able arms, and took her to bed. She held him close, "What was I worried about?" He thought, "she loves me."

From John's mind, weeks came and so did a familiar chill resurfaced in his body. "Does she still love me? Why doesn't she seem happy? I am not flying on long international assignments. I am testing, training young officers at Dobbs Air Force Base. I got what we wanted; she doesn't seem interested in being an officer's wife. I'll try to give her some time. I wish I didn't feel compressed, separated from her heart. Our love making is not the same; she does not smile so much."

That Tuesday evening, in October, they were enjoying John's home-made sangria. The record player played, Duke Ellington's "In a Sentimental Mood." They held hands on the front porch. John told stories about his friend Handsome Joe. "Baby," she said. "Why don't we take a trip to Louisiana, and visit with Joe and his family this year." She held his hands; John kissed hers, as they swayed on the hanging lounger.

The next morning was a quiet breakfast: salmon cakes, buttery grits, cheese-eggs, and watermelon. "Baby, I think, I'll visit with Miss May this week-end." Megan went back to reading *Creative Loafing*. John ceased reading the *Atlanta Constitution*, "City Elects First Black Mayor." He stared at her melancholy eyes. "Okay, Baby."

Her white oval overnight suitcase was packed before noon on Friday. She didn't kiss John goodbye. She drove free in her white convertible Mustang. He went in the kitchen and dialed Miss May Perry. "Megan is on her way for the weekend, could you call me when she arrives. Her car needs a check-up; I want to make sure she arrives okay." He hung up the phone, opened the refrigerator, grabbed two Carlsberg beers, and speeded to their bedroom. A half an hour later, he stuck his head in John Jr.'s room, grinned at the towering poster of Bill Russell.

"Let me call my son, check up on him."

Megan drove to Miss May Perry's property, followed behind cherry blossoms tress, and a storm of engine smoke. The car dragged in the circular driveway to the colonial-style house. She hustled out. "Miss May, I'm so glad to see you, My God, I thought my car was going to blow up, but I wasn't afraid."

"Child, come in the house. Your husband has been calling, worried sick about you."

After his beers, bags of salted peanuts, John had a big sized headache. He fell asleep while reading the October 15, *Sports Illustrated* magazine, "Tiny Archibald Does It All." He awoke an hour and half later when the telephone rang at two o'clock, and he murmured, "Hello," his head pounding.

"John," Miss May Perry, said "Megan arrived and she is fine."

"Can I speak to her Miss May?"

"John she is lying down, I'll have her call you after her rest."

"Don't worry, she will be just fine, and back home with her man."

"I know." John's hand was on his head, the other on his stomach. "Take care of her for me."

"Don't I always, son?"

20

When he was seven years old, John hid under his bed during rain storms, roaring thunder, warnings of tornados. After, he became a fighter pilot, weather never mattered. He lost the fear of storms, at least of nature. Nevertheless, he was not in his cockpit, he was in his house, and he trotted to the basement for his tool box. He hit his head on the low ceiling. Within seconds, he brushed next to the square, rustic chest of handyman supplies. At the same time, the lights came back on in the house. "This always happens; I should remember to wait for a few minutes, but I can't."

For two days, Megan had not returned his calls. Miss May Perry repeated the same word, "she resting." He turned the basement light out and entered the empty kitchen. The storm on Chester Street had ended, the hunger for her had not. "This is a minor distraction; comfort is on the way." He opened the refrigerator and grasped two "lager beers; he grilled two rare cheeseburgers and relaxed in the family room, watching the basketball game on WAGA-TV.

Around one in the afternoon at Miss May Perry's house, Megan rolled out of bed and brushed her frizzy hair. It was tangled; she used her fingers to loosen it, strand by strand.

"No rush," she mumbled. "Nobody to care for," she hesitated. "No Big Boy Blue."

"At Last," an Etta James song, played in her room on Saturday morning, Saturday night, and Sunday morning. Megan rolled over in bed to play the song again. Miss May Perry burst in her guest room and turned the record player off. Megan didn't utter a sound. Miss May slammed the door.

"Is this who I am?" She surveyed her image in the rectangular brass mirror: her peach chiffon gown was wrinkled; Maybelline brown mascara soiled her cheeks. She slogged back to bed.

She pulled the linen sheet over her head. "I will get up today; I need another hour to rest. Oh God, help me not to think. When I think I cry, and when I cry I stay in bed."

Big and strong, quick and fast, Blue Bedford ran across the massive Ohio Stadium. He was working out, testing his speed, training for a well-rounded game. He saw students glaring, gleeful about the player they read about in *The Columbus Dispatch* and saw on WPBO-TV.

"Hey Blue," the assistant coach said. "I saw you running out there; even in the rain your speed is powerful. I like the way you are working. Let's see what you can do tomorrow."

"My strength is growing," Blue, buried in his thoughts. "I held myself back at Eden High. College ball is professional ball, a money train. Everything, I ever wanted I got, but you, Megan, I don't have you."

The rain was reinvigorating, he opened his lungs, "Muddy fucking day; it's the same every day." He stopped running; he tied his athletic shoes tighter, picked-up his speed; sprinkles became a downpour. He rested underneath the stone alcove adjacent to the locker rooms.

He watched the rain fall. Quietly, he said, "Remember the poem, I wrote to you, Baby?"

"The sky looked like that the day I saw you, and it was easy to love you then as I still do. It was misty grey, mighty blue, Big Boy Blue can't stop wanting to love you." It was then you gave yourself to me, our hearts became one.

He walked to the shower, her smell with him. "I won't call you anymore," he said. "Not this minute," he laughed.

On another green field, there was a knock at the door. Miss May Perry gently opened the bronze door. "Megan, when you put some clothes on, come down for lunch," She said, staring at her bare body. "There are no men in the house to run around naked." She shut the door.

Megan stepped out of bed, wrapped her chenille robe around her waist, and searched for pen and paper in Miss Mays' dresser drawer. Sitting on the French settee, she wrote words to Blue: *I miss our love lost. When you touch me, I can't breathe, but don't stop. Some say love is temporary, home is peace, love, our love, is it lost?* She crossed out the words in black ink and wrote: *John Jr. loves his father, they are friends. Who do I have? Blue. Do I love Blue?* Urgently, her hands ripped the paper in shreds.

Upright on the off-white settee, she stared at the iron and brass sleigh bed. "Whenever, John and I stay overnight, this is our bedroom. The French rattan, antique finish, smooth curves, and iron handles held the closeness of our lovemaking. John joked with Miss May Perry about her travels in Europe.

Miss May said right after her husband died in 1962, she boarded a plane to Paris, France. People followed her around France thinking she was an exotic jazz singer. "I kept explaining," she laughed, "I was not Josephine Baker." Four weeks of shopping, and I became bored. I soon realized, men were chasing my money and not honey."

Megan made up the bed; she dressed in a rose cotton dress, stared in the long floor mirror. "John, what happened to us? How could you keep a secret about John Jr. and West Point from me?" she paused, "How could I?"

"Why am I here? I left John at home to think about Blue? No, that's not true. I left home, because, I don't love my husband."

In her trance, Megan thought of her father. "Why did you stop loving my mother? What did Lina do to lose your love?"

"Megan, lunch is getting cold," she heard Miss May say.

She hurried to the kitchen and kissed Miss May Perry's heavily powered cheeks. Megan looked at her shrimp and spinach salad. Miss May stared at her messy hair.

"You're so judgmental, Megan," Miss May said. "Why? You judge your husband, your son, maybe me too. Why can't you appreciate you have a man at home who loves you, who would die for you if he had to. Perhaps, your son decided not to go to Morehouse, but he's doing something good with his life. You want to blame your men for your worries. Are they judging you for sleeping with that boy? And don't think they don't know—your husband suspects something is different.

"I saw how your son looked at you at his graduation party. He was talking to his father. He abruptly looked at you and saw your frightened face. He walked over to the screen door; you were standing mute, looking at that boy. I intercepted your husband to distract him; he senses something is wrong. And now, his fear of losing you has come. My God, who knows what he has been through flying those airplanes. I know one thing; he has come back alive because of you. Do you think he is not man enough to fight for you?"

She listened, held her coffee, and surveyed the space in Miss May's kitchen. "It's larger than my living room, and she never cooks. Miss Esther, her live-in maid, cook, companion keeps the floors sparking white. Her hand-made countertop from Charlotte, North Carolina, the black mahogany table was shipped from Italy and..."

"Megan," she said. "Do you hear me, child?"

"Yes," I was thinking of strolling on your grounds; you know how much I love your rolling acres of high trees."

"What about your lunch? Miss Esther thought you would like something simple."

"I'm not hungry right now. May I have it later?"

Miss Esther walked in. "Miss May Perry, it is Mr. John Smith again calling to speak to Mrs. Smith."

She leaped out of her chair. "Miss Esther, could you tell Mr. Smith I've gone for a walk, and I'll telephone him in a little while."

Miss May Perry watched Megan strolled toward her enormous cherry tree. "Miss Esther, I'm thinking about cutting down that tree; people are always wandering over there."

"What do I tell Mr. Smith, Miss May Perry?"

"Yes, tell him his wife is wandering."

By the time Megan returned to the house, her salad was soggy, and she cut some peaches in a bowl. She was about to sit down.

"Megan, you had a telephone call," Miss May said abruptly.

"Did you tell John, I'll call him right back," she said anxiously.

"No," she said, "It was someone named Big Boy Blue. I told him you were resting."

They glared in each other's confident eyes. "Yes," Megan said. "I am resting." Miss May Perry smiled; Megan went outside.

Taking his time, the following morning, John awoke late. He was not on military time, but Megan's time. His sturdy strong arms touched her empty pillow. "She's been away for almost three days; perhaps, she's run away from home."

The fall leaves, the flowing breeze, reminded him of the moments before he proposed marriage to her. "Today is the day she is coming home." He grabbed his long-sleeved cotton white shirt and house shoes and stormed to the kitchen.

He opened the refrigerator: one dozen eggs, salted butter, one bottle of milk, half pound of Guatemalan coffee. "Where's the bread? I guess my wife didn't have time to think about groceries, she was too giddy driving away."

The neighbors' Doberman pinscher was barking at the mailman. "I forgot to check the mail box. He scurried out of the house; his black jeans were loose. "I must have lost five pounds."

Leaves were disbursed throughout the front yard, the grass overflowed into Mrs. Rose's property. "I got to do landscaping today. He circled around his red Mustang. "My Pony needs a wash." The mail box was full of magazines: *Ebony*, "Hank Aaron Catching Up With 'The Babe,'" *Small Air Force Observer*, *Mustang Monthly*, *Gourmet*, *The Atlanta Constitution*. "Nothing, but magazines," he said. "Wait a minute—a letter from West Baton Rouge, Louisiana." He grinned wide, "Handsome Joe, my buddy."

John smiled sensing good news from Joe. He surveyed the yard again and said, "Coffee first, letter second, Megan third, and the landscaping tomorrow."

He tossed the magazines on the white marble coffee table. Fifteen minutes flew by, coffee in his right hand, Joe's letter in the other. He headed to his bedroom and relaxed in the wing chair. He grabbed his hand-made letter-opener and read:

Dear John,

I'm sitting back looking at my life, thought I'll write a letter to my friend, my brother. I was thinking how it was midnight blue the morning I arrived in New York on Saturday, November 13, 1954. Not long after the Korean War, I received an honorable discharge. The commander said, "Joe, at best, your shakes comes and goes, and makes you unreliable."

If my skills as a fighter pilot were gone, I wanted out. You know, I'm grateful you convinced me to start corresponding with my mother, Margaret. She pleaded for me to move to Baton Rouge, Louisiana. I had no other family, but I had to find Suzy Mae.

How ironic for me to receive letters from my mother, not Suzy Mae. Every letter I sent to her was marked returned, no reply. In my last letter, I asked her to marry me if she still loved me. I had been living at Mrs. Hollins' rooming house on 136th and Eighth Avenue; I figure I could hang around for a few weeks before my money ran out.

Man, women were here and there chasing me down, telling me how handsome I was, what they could give me. I was tempted; thankfully, Mrs. Hollins didn't allow women in her house. Old routines became familiar: Saturday nights at Small's Paradise on 135th Street and Seventh Avenue. I caught up with former college buddies and saw a few street dudes I didn't want to see. But, I settled in at the bar listening to a jazz band, smoking my Camel cigarettes. Time took over; I was drinking vodka straight-up, finally deciding to leave during the last set. Then, a pretty, light-skinned girl with thin hair moved in close. "Is your name Handsome Joe?" she asked. I thought, "She ain't that pretty." But I asked, "Why do you want to know?"

W. D. Moore

"My name is Gladys; I know your woman, Suzy Mae." My husband is up there playing the trombone, Cecil Sparks— he knows Suzy; but I know where she lives."

I put my cigarette out, her man watched me. "Well pretty lady, tell me, where I can find her?"

Sunday morning at eight o'clock, I was waiting on Brandhurst and 152nd Street. Suzy, walked out of a white brownstone holding a little girl's hands. Her freckles and fine body were exactly how I remembered. The exception was flaming-red straight hair was shoulder-length curls. My only disappointment, I couldn't see her earlobes, so I touched her ear and she smiled.

"Hello Suzy Mae." She touched my older face.

"Hello Handsome Joe."

"Mommy, who is that man?" Suzy laughed, "Josephina, he is your daddy." They were on their way to Sunday school on Convent Avenue but did not make it. We went to Ideal Restaurant where we first met on 145th Street. We had breakfast and talked through lunch. She cooked dinner, we played with Josephina. My daughter refused to go to sleep, and then at eleven o'clock at night, she dropped out cold in my lap. Suzy and I made love; we were competing to see who would die first.

Within seven days, my five-year-old daughter, Suzy Mae, and I moved to Louisiana. We were married in my momma's back yard.

Margaret was not pleased about the marriage. Josephina was another story. She played with her granddaughter, she brushed her hair, and granddaughter helped grand-mamma in the kitchen. Suddenly, home felt like real home.

Two more children later, I kept thinking about that character Skeeter at Mather Air Force Base. Remember the guys joking with him about his wife? He said, "I can't stand that woman; she eats my food, sleeps in my bed, and treats me like crap." "Man, why don't you get rid of her?" I asked. He shot back, "What, you mean, Joe? How can I get rid of something I love?"

That's how I felt about Suzy Mae; Margaret was not being nice to her 'cause she was white. I told momma we were leaving. You know, Margaret is a good-looking woman; she thinks she is twenty-five; she gets a bit jealous of Suzy Mae. But on Mother's Day, my momma, tall, sharp-witted at sixty-five-years old, cozy up in her rocking chair on the veranda, in her hand was an envelope. "Here, I want to give you the deed to my house. We are family; I want to make sure you don't go away.

My attorney, Miss Yasmin Scott, says my spacious, three-story house, five bedrooms, one acre of land is worth a lot of money. I told her, what I need money for, when I got love around me. Miss Scott is a handsome, dark-skinned woman with an enchanting smile, from Trinidad. "I'm not worried about you 'caused you are in love. Right, son?" Margaret stood straight, hands on her hip, rolled her eyes. I kissed her rouge cheeks, she chuckled.

I won't kid you, John; Suzy Mae became a prisoner of my mind. I loved her long ago, all the time, since the beginning. I used to challenge you about finding a woman that loves you. My friend let me tell you: I learned you can't let her go, there's no guarantee you can get her back."

By the way, when are we getting our families together? Suzy Mae was thinking perhaps, one Christmas holiday. Would you ask Megan? Anyway, I figured if we can survive Korea, we can schedule the time. I know you were the leader pilot, and I was your wingman, but now I am gonna be the leader and tell you to ask your wife about Christmas. Hey, we need to sit down with a drink, be dazzled by our women, and demand they let us have one cigarette.

Got to run brother, we love you, guys. Joe.

P.S., Can you believe, my two sons are at the Air Force Academy in Colorado Springs, and John Jr. is a West Point Cadet? We are damn lucky. Joe.

John read Joe's letter again. His stomach thumped; he missed her taste, her touch. He dialed Miss May Perry's number.

"Hello, I need to speak to my wife, now, Miss May."

"Certainly," she said and moved fast.

Wide-eyed, Megan was awake, staring at the sunlight; her mind danced with Big Boy Blue.

"Your husband is on the phone; he is not asking you to come to the phone. He told me to bring you to the phone."

"Tell him I'll call him when I am ready."

"Child, you must decide this moment if you want your man or not. This man wants you now, and if you don't come to the telephone, I know he will never call again. You can't stay and live in my home forever. It's been three days—he's not waiting for another. I tell you something, he is a patient man. If you want to give up twenty years of good loving for a know nothing, then you go ahead. Get up, get to it, Megan; you are no longer a child. Stop feeling sorry for yourself. Save yourself while you can. You can't have that big boy, and there's nothing you can do about it. What are you going to do?"

Whatever Megan saw in Miss May Perry's eyes, it forced her body out of the bed. She swiftly chased the telephoned in bare feet on the Persian runner to Miss May's room.

"Hello John." She inhaled.

"Hey Baby, I'm coming today to bring you home, I'll be there in two hours," he said, and he clicked the phone.

She looked at her wedding-band finger, recognized the ring was not there. She hadn't paid it no mind all this time. "Oh, look at my nails."

"Well, tell me what did you choose?"

"I didn't; he chose for me. He didn't wait for an answer."

She clapped her hands. "You spoke to a captain in the United States Air Force, your husband, your true man. Well, child, you have done gone and become a woman. Esther will cook us a big lunch this afternoon. I know your John is gonna be mighty hungry, driving from Atlanta. You best get dressed; look prettier than Esther's homemade butter biscuits. Hurry up, so you can set the table."

White teeth, bright smiles, Megan's squeezed Miss May Perry tight.

"Child, I can't breathe," she said. "Esther, where are you?"

"Right here, Miss Perry," she nodded.

"Sorry, I didn't see you in the hallway. We're having company coming for lunch." She looked at Megan.

"Child, I declare, you are your Momma's Georgia peach."

As always, John checked his radio clock by his military watch. Each confirmed it was eleven o'clock. "This feels like a day and time of yesterday. The grey sky, the misty rain, the telephone didn't ring when I needed peace. Let me get ready."

He hiked into the bathroom, shaved slowly, and patted his crew haircut. "I'm glad I went to Mo's Barber's last Saturday." He glanced at the radio, turned it to WAOK.

"Listen up Atlanta," the disc jockey said. "All day we are playing Marvin Gaye and Tammi Terrell. If you missed your favorite song, don't worry; we are playing an encore at midnight. Sit back, lay back, I'll be back to your calls after the next song." John stepped in the shower, sang along to "Your Precious Love."

In the warm water, he reminiscence, "In our years, I never grasped the danger of days of being away from her, losing Megan. When I spotted her, she captivated my soul.

Her seductive beauty, voluptuous breast, Venus body kept me up at night, until I married her. I dreamed about her when I was not thinking about her; I was in danger.

"She, being a young girl at eighteen, I was twenty-eight, I didn't care, why should I? I was smitten the second she walked in the Royal Peacock Club. It was pure luck I was there in September. I had landed in Atlanta from Korea, 1953. Although the war officially ended on July 27th, I was not planning to leave Korea. The commander reassigned me back to the United States the first of September. I could not wait for a long courtship because I was due in Eastern Europe by February 27, 1954.

"For the first time, I examined myself. Have I found something I need more than flying? I was attractive to Megan, astonished at how much I wanted her.

"After hours of tossing, turning, waiting for the early sun rise, the next day, we were to meet for lunch at Paschal's Restaurant on West Hunter Street.

"'It's the best Southern food in Atlanta,' she said. I couldn't keep my heart from pounding; I puzzled over, 'Could I be falling in love?' I kept preaching to my brain, I don't need this now; I thought about her essence, her everything I desired. I started smoking like smoking Joe.

"The night we danced, I could have cut open my heart for a kiss; her baby lips, smooth-looking skin, silky hair. How could I suffer this pain another night, I wondered. I will have to marry her. Defeat was not an option, determination would prevail, I would have Megan in my bed for the rest of my life."

He dried himself off, stared at her portrait over the fireplace. "I gave you too much time to decide what was best for our family. I felt guilty leaving you home to raise John Jr. Yes, our son is a West Point Cadet. The family is changing; we are still a family."

He opened the dresser, dressed in his underwear, and relaxed on the bed. "She stays firm, fresh in my eyes. This minute, I want her more than a child's craving for breast milk. It will take me an hour drive to Macon, an hour at Miss May Perry's house, an hour back home. I hope I can wait that long."

He made up their pearl linen bed, afterwards the telephone rang, "Hello?" A hard click. Another second, there was another ring.

"Hello?" The same click.

"What the hell is going on? Could someone be calling for Megan? He fastened his watch, and the telephoned rang. "Who the fuck is this?" he yelled.

"Baby," Megan said sweetly. "Is this how you answer the telephone when I am not there?"

"Megan, I'm sorry. It rang twice, and there was no one on the other line. It doesn't matter. I'm leaving in a ten minutes to pick you up."

"Baby, hurry, bring me home," her shivering voice said.

"Megan, what's going on Baby? We are too old for secrets. Why did you stay away from me? I missed you. I will be there shortly."

Her sultry voice said, "Baby, I was angry about John Jr. These days from you have helped me to realize I had to let my son go. Can you appreciate what my life has been, waiting for you to come home all this time?"

"Baby, I home now." "I know, John, hurry up. Miss May is sick of her house guest."

He laughed. "Be there soon."

"Ain't No Mountain High Enough," played on the radio. He turned up the volume, singing, humming. In the mirror, the camel cardigan, cotton trousers pleased him. He bolted down the stairs in black loafers. A moment passed; he jogged back to his bedroom.

"Thanks, WAOK, I can take care of it from here." The radio was off, and so was he.

21

Just as a bird that fears a cat, Megan's heart raced to the toilet, and she vomited. "Blue, how can I stop him? He is making his presence known. My desire for him is over; he is not more important than John, my family.

"Why did I have to almost lose John to want him? Let me take a long bath and bring back my husband to me." A clear-headed Megan was certain about her love, after her bath; she sprayed Miss May Perry's Yves Saint Laurent perfume at John's special places. "I plan to wear a different dress."

Miss May Perry entered the bedroom and admired her beauty. "Megan, you are absolutely stunning, and the older you get the more beautiful you are like your mother. Do you remember your mother's glow? What happened when your father no longer adored her? Lina was never the same. What will you do when John finds out about that big boy? Will he want you? Will you risk it? Will you take that risk?

"I know one thing—I won't bother to tell Esther to prepare dinner. John will be in a hurry to rush you home. Any day is a long time for a hungry man to wait, especially if he does not have to."

Applying her light pink lipstick, "He sounds the same. He still loves me, and I love him."

"Good, because a young man name "Big Boy Blue," is on hold to speak to you."

Her lipstick slipped out of her hand. Her motionless body was like a frozen rivulet.

"Megan, end this relationship before your husband arrives. Can you? Can you release your desire for this big boy? Who do you love?"

A meteorologist would call it ice raindrops descending down her face. "Now look at you; your face is ruined. You will have to redo it. Go on and use the telephone in my bedroom. Tell him, Megan, it is over."

Trudging across the hallway, she was swept away in a moment of terrifying fear. She stared at the black "trimline" telephone on the art deco nightstand. She paused and closed the door. "Hello Blue."

His stomach growled. "Baby, I've been crazy trying to find you. I telephoned your house, and remembered your aunt. She told me you couldn't come to the phone, but I knew you would. I can't work out; I can't eat; all I want is you. I got to be with you. What's wrong Baby? When can I see you?"

"Blue, my husband is on his way to take me home. He can't find out about us. I can't see you anymore."

"He doesn't have to find out about us. I can fly to Atlanta; you can fly out here, anytime. I love you, and I know you love me. His hands will never give you my kind of love. You know you want me, Baby, you know it. Say it, and I won't call you anymore. Just say you don't want me, I will let you go."

Her voice was soft, and her heart was strong. He relaxed on his bed, staring at the white sky. Megan sat upright on a black chaise longue. "Blue, I do not want you to call my house or my aunt's home ever again. I don't love you."

He leaped off the bed and stood mightier than a bald eagle. "You can't say you don't want me. And, Baby, I know you love me; I love you. Okay, I won't call you; you will have to call me. When you do, and you will, I won't be tender like before. I will be painful. Hey Baby, maybe that's the way you always wanted it." The telephone clicked. He had tears in his eyes; one dropped.

His Warrior wings circled around the room, he flopped in a chair, head pressed down. His left knee began to ache; he stretched his large thighs, holding both iron arms against the wall. The pain continued. He pushed his Greek literature and world history books on the floor, resting his leg on the desk, holding the chair firm. "Money," he hollered, "I just need money. If she would wait until I start pro ball in two years, she can divorce her husband and be with me." He reached for a bottle of aspirins, took four out. Immediately, he crushed them and threw the bottle on the floor. "Don't start taking drugs; how the hell will you control your body?" He sat in the chair and elevated his knee, thinking of a plan.

In Miss May Perry's bedroom, Megan imagined Blue's hands were beating her heart with a sledgehammer. There was no escape. Instantly, she touched her heart, and it was there, and he was not. She shivered, lost her posture; her sleek body crawled on the floor. She prayed, "The lord is my Shepherd, I shall not want." Tears of dead roses tramp her heart. Miss May Perry opened the door and stared in disbelief.

"Megan, get up—get dressed. I will try to stop your husband from coming up these stairs, because if he sees you like this he will know and leave you forever." She turned away, closed the door; and started walking down the staircase. The door bell rang again and again.

"John is going to tear my door down to get his woman. If he rings it one more time, Lord, get these young folks away from me.

"John, you are here. Come on in and give your Aunt May a big hug." He handed her a passionflower and hugged her like his mother. "That's the best welcome I have had my entire life."

"Aunt May, where is everybody?"

Her sapphire diamonds sparkled in his eyes; he stared in her pink eyes. "Now, you know we weren't going to rush to open my door. It's good to have a man anxious for his woman."

He switched his clear eyes above her oak, wooden staircase. "Miss May Perry, where's Megan?"

"John, go in the kitchen, Esther will give you some coffee. I'll bring her downstairs. Megan is getting dress real pretty for you. You know how long she can be.

"Esther has been frying red snapper, stir-fried spinach with garlic, and olive oil. Don't get me started with the coconut cake she baked early this morning, when I asked her to make a simple butter pound cake. And don't think I'm gonna waste money, Esther's time, my mind trying to figure out what you like. Son, your wife is not leaving this house except with you, let her have her entrance." He kissed Miss May Perry on the cheeks.

"I know you are like a momma to both of us; we love you Miss May. That coffee sure smells good; I bet you baked my favorite buttery biscuits too."

"Son, you know Esther did."

They walked together to the kitchen; John held her arm.

"I was checking Megan's car in the driveway; I'm going to have my buddy repair her 289 engine, drive it back to our home. I bought her convertible from Chestnut Spriggs, he owns Spriggs' Mustang Shop in Macon.

"Spriggs was an ace aircraft mechanic in Korea. He can repair anything on land or in the air. His true love is Mustang convertibles. He is recognizable by his hazel-green eyes. Ladies, call him Dream Heart, be careful—you might fall in love."

"John, you mean to tell me this today. I could have had your friend over every day for lunch. I am just sick of surprises around here; let me go bring your wife down before you eat everything in my kitchen."

He giggled, "Not everything I want to eat is in the kitchen."

"Son, sit down, stay right here."

On her way, she took her time walking to Megan. Buried in her thoughts, Miss May Perry recollected, "When I was a young girl, I was told my best feature was my hands, handsome, some say, elegant others said. I soaked them in warm water in the mornings, cold water at night. Every Saturday afternoon, manicures, pedicures; and monthly facials. I admitted to Esther once, It makes me feel like a young girl. Esther smiled, stared at her working hands, and covered them behind her uniform.

"Today, for whatever reason, I feel older than seventy-two; it's the same feeling whenever Megan comes over to visit. She reminds me what I don't have, never had. She has been more of a daughter than an adopted niece. She has what women, rich or not, will never know about. Love from a man, being adored by a man. Now she has two men wanting her. I don't need this agony in my bones right now. And the risk she takes—I can't believe. I need to get away, travel to a faraway place, where men will look at me a spell, and if I have to pay for it, well, I'll think about that later."

She eyed her hands. "They are not as beautiful as a girl of twenty or a woman of forty, but there's nothing I can do about it. All the expensive nail polish, massages, and pampering don't make a difference." Her hands guided her heavy thoughts to Megan's room.

In her aunt's home, Megan stood certain, staring through the burgundy draperies at the trees and the lake where she watched Canadian Geese. In the front were the father, and then the mother, and two children-geese followed. Watching their family brought love to her heart and happiness for her own. "What is it about nature? Perhaps, it's full of love and removes loneliness of the heart. It's regal—life refuses to be deprived." She turned to the chocolate armoire, changed into a red bell-sleeve jersey dress. Miss May Perry's hands were on the door knob; she gently closed it.

She reached for Megan's hands. "I remember what it was like to be touched by a man. The madness I got from him was not worth being with him. At first he was kind, good; he treated me like no one could. As soon as I started standing up for myself, he forced his way on me. I'm not talking physically. He played mental games to ensure his control over me. I was twenty-eight, he whispered nightly how I was nothing, nobody would ever want me, and he did not know why he wanted me. I hated his touch, I hated my weakness for him, and I hated myself.

"I ran away; he found me and promised he would be kinder. But he was mean because he loved me and didn't want me to go. In my heart, I knew I could not trust him; I stayed another month. He continued to say horrible words to me. I packed and put his key in the mail box. Lina, your mother, let me stay with her, until I could make some sense of my life. That's why I loved your momma, and I love you. I was with him for six years; I looked at myself in the mirror and said, there you are, thank God, you are still here. You think that big boy wants to be with you forever, or just whenever. I couldn't say, I do know your husband is downstairs and truly loves you. You can take him for granted if you want to, but you are a fool if you do. He is young to me; when you are over seventy everyone becomes young.

"This man will stay with you in the morning, afternoon, and every night. Megan, I may not be here for you to run away from home anymore. Before your mother left this world, she asked me to help you, to teach you, give you what I gave her: unconditional love. You know, your mother listened to me; she and I were the same age, and she was a married woman. She treated me like an older sister. Lina was cautious; she liked security. Your parents, especially your father spoiled you; your mother taught you the Southern attributes a woman can be to a man. Megan, your real man, your husband for close to twenty years is downstairs waiting for his wife. Do you think he would be there if he knew about that boy? Do you think he would want you anymore? Do you think he would forgive you, see you the same?

"Don't be stupid, don't risk everything for nothing. And if he calls you, hang up the phone. If he knocks on your door, don't open it. And be certain when I say, never tell your husband.

"Now, sugar child, come down stairs; let there be no doubts to your man that you are his lady."

Four hands of love became one; they huddled as sisters. Megan moved to brush her hair and turned and walked back to Miss May Perry. She hugged her closer.

"What are you and your husband trying to do to me? I'm a small old lady; I can't take this foolishness forever. Hurry up child, food is on the table."

"I'll be right down Aunt May." She danced over to the dressing table, reclined in her chair and slipped her wedding band on. She reached for the red nail polish. "This will take too long to dry." She applied clear color. "When I get home, I'll shine my ring, John's too, if I can get him to take it off."

22

Joys of good-hearted laughter soaked the kitchen when her red toes hit the pink tile floor. "I hope you saved some coffee for me," Megan's pale pink lips said. "Knowing my husband, I'll have to make another pot."

In his hand, he tasted the French vanilla blend, staring at her every movement. The dress demonstrated her curves; it clung tight, fitted right. The suppleness of her breasts announced the attraction to come. Silk stockings were not visible. In pain, he wondered, "What about lace panties." Rive Gauche perfume directed his eyes to her graceful hands, when she touched her neck, her lips. "I'm being educated: She is mine; he is hers to have."

He continued to be captivated, "Her subtle ballet movements are bringing memories of Duke Ellington's "Hot and Bothered." One night she gave it to me on our bedroom floor. She whispered, 'are you bothered baby?' We bothered each other, until our three-year-old son came in the bedroom crying. We held hands, John Jr. laid beside his mother's chest; I settled underneath her breasts; everyone slept on the daisy rug." Megan smiled at John; he remained in a trance: "The smell of her shampoo, takes me to our honeymoon night, when she became my woman. I washed her hair in the bathtub, carried her to the bed, we loved each other for two days without leaving the house."

In the deepness of his desire he said, "Can I make it until we finished this meal? If I could take her up stairs, love her, if Miss May Perry needed to visit a friend urgently, if Miss Esther had taken the day off. I should have run up those stairs and loved her for lunch.

"I don't remember anything this painful to my body, not even when I almost died in Korea. I must be patient; everybody knows my will. This moment I need help; Miss May could you go shopping and take Esther with you?"

In her alluring hands, Megan held the porcelain cup and faced John. "Baby, do you want more red snapper?" He stared at the tip of her lips.

"No Megan," he replied.

"Are you sure?" she asked.

W. D. Moore

Miss Esther had laid a pot of freshly brewed coffee on the table, while serving, it spilled on her hand. "Ouch," she said.

Tense eyes met, husband and wife set on each other. "What could be keeping Miss May Perry?" Esther nervously said. "I think I'll let her know her lunch is getting nipple...I mean nippy."They smiled.

"Excuse me." Esther went out in a hurry.

He sat his fork on the table, went to the stone countertop, and cut a slice of coconut cake. She moved close to him. "Baby, do you like Esther's cake better than mine?" she enquired, standing closer.

"No, it's not better than yours. I prefer your cake." John said, and placed the dish down. Megan kissed his fresh coconut lips.

"I'm sorry I waited to come home."

"We are not home yet." She became somber.

"Why sad eyes, we love each other. Our son will be fine, you raised him, and he is strong because of you." Her full waves embraced his chest; he drew her in closer. They kissed, he rubbed her behind. "She's not wearing panties," John thought, kissing her neck, back to her lips again.

"If you two don't sit down," Miss May Perry said. "I've been preparing this luncheon all morning, Miss Esther, where the heck is you?" She stumbled in, stepped on Miss May Perry's foot. "Ouch," Miss May hollered. "Let's eat so these married folks can go home."

The Smiths held hands while laughing about John Jr. getting lost in New York's Grand Central station. Miss May Perry laughed. Miss Esther poured pink lemonade in a Waterford crystal pitcher; she did not laugh.

23

Just as John predicted I-75 into Atlanta was bumper to bumper traffic at five-thirty. The first thirty minutes was an easy breeze, forty-five minutes later, a Dairy Queen truck hit a red Volvo. Vehicles were honking, drivers shouting expletives. Megan's eyes were closed. She held John's right hand; he drove with his left. She crossed her legs and slipped off her shoes. John kissed her hand. Minutes passed, he saw an opening and took it, off I-20. In fifteen seconds he turned and swirled on Peachtree Street.

His vision pierced at the tallest building downtown, the Hyatt Regency. She opened her eyes. "Baby, what are you doing?" John's Pony entered the Blue Dome. "John, we are ten minutes from home."

"Not if we stayed on the expressway, no way we would be home; besides, I can't wait." He handed the attendant his car keys. They checked in, her eyes gazed at the glass elevator, he pushed ten. She said to herself, "This is where we celebrated our second wedding anniversary. It's been years since we cuddled here."

John squeezed Megan's hand and opened the door. The room was decorated in blue fabric chairs. Her mind murmured, "I don't feel a blue bone in my body."

His hands wrapped around her waist. "Did you remember to wear your panties, Baby?" She stood against the door; his raw hand eased inside.

"I knew you couldn't wait," she whispered in his ear.

An early, quiet morning, I-20 was perfect traffic. He wanted to rest longer; she wanted her own bed. They held hands walking in their home. "Oh, my God," Megan said staggeringly. "What happened to our house? I was only gone for a few days; look at our home."

He guided her hand upstairs; she strolled to her vanity. He unclasped the pearl clip from her hair; his hands rubbed her back. She turned and faced him.

"I want more, I need more," he said. She guided him to their bed and gave him lots more, up to the beat of his breath slowed down.

W. D. Moore

She awoke at noon; John slept. She tiptoed out of bed and grabbed his white, long-sleeved shirt. She wanted coffee, breakfast. She slipped on her puffy pink slippers and skipped to the kitchen. There she scrambled six eggs in the cast-iron skillet and brewed Guatemalan coffee. She peeked through the embroidered white curtains. "The past is gone; the future is here with my husband."

He glanced at his watch, called her name, "Megan." Not quite a half a minute, she with his button-down shirt open, silver tray in hand, displaying her God-given gifts. His eyes enamored her essence, her everything.

"Baby, are you trying to kill me?" He smiled.

"I want you strong, Baby." She clutched the large spoon.

"This must be heaven," he thought. They loved as one: husband and wife, lovers and friends, mother and father, all over again.

The next few months, the Smiths, their backyard became a Garden of Megan. John planted magnolia trees; she planted marigold, roses, and fleabanes. They both planted a vegetable garden. Summer evenings were barbecues with other officers and their families. Megan joined a bird-watching women's club on Sundays. She became engrossed with vermilion flycatchers, scissor-tailed flycatchers. John displayed his handyman skills: built new bird houses outside the kitchen and bedroom windows.

Vacations were centered on their hobbies: hiking, bird watching, fly fishing, golf, and nights by the ocean making love.

It was January 1975; their family life blossomed like the change of seasons and each season got better. John's forty-ninth birthday was February 1st. A month before the celebration, Megan decided to surprise him with a new television set. She drove his "Pony" to Rich's Department Store on Fulton Street.

Rich's parking lot was filled to capacity; she was lucky, squeezed in a space on the ground level. "Oh, how perfect, I don't have to walk too far with my shopping bags," she exclaimed. She stepped out. At the same time, a tall tailored man was spellbound at the powder-blue, velvet, two-piece suit. "It's two o'clock, I'm only buying John's gift. I'm promising myself to be home by five o'clock to start dinner."

The first floor was her favorite; her eyes gazed for her girl at the Estée Lauder cosmetic counter. "I could stay here forever," she thought. She received a complimentary make-up demonstration. An hour later, she said, "Helen, it's getting late, and I can't decide."

Her brown alligator heels steered up to the second floor, ladies Lingerie. She saw a mannequin in a red satin night gown. "Miss," said she. "Do you have this gown in pink and purple in a size six?"

"Yes, Ma'am, we do, I'll be right back." The gold-leaf wall clock showed the time was three-thirty when the sales lady returned. "Your dressing room is ready; I also brought some other designs in your size that you might like."

"Thank you. Could you also bring me that short, black-chiffon robe?"

She tried on six gowns. The sales lady stopped by her room. "Is there anything else you would like to see, Ma'am?"

"Yes, what floor is the entertainment department on?"

Her half-smile and sunken eyes muttered, "The fifth floor. Are you sure you don't like even one gown, Ma'am?"

"I'm sure, but could you hold them for me until tomorrow. My name is Mrs. John Smith."

"Yes, Mrs. Smith, I will."

Roundabout four-thirty; Megan reached in her alligator handbag and held on to her Rich's credit card. Glowing Estée Lauder eyes surveyed the televisions. A salesman approached, "Good afternoon, Ma'am. May I help you with our products today?"

"Yes, I would like to buy a television for my husband, but there are so many choices. I know he wants a twenty-four inch, but they all look the same to me."

The short, slick-haired salesman made a Motown smile. "He looks likes Same Cooke," Megan thought.

"Follow me, Ma'am; my wife bought me this RCA twenty-four inch for my birthday yesterday. I love it."

Instantly, other customers began to cheer and clap. Another second, hands were in the air. Every television was tuned to the Rose Bowl college football game. The salesman's head swerved away from Megan. "Can you believe that guy from the Ohio State Buckeyes? Just like that USC Trojans could have lost the game." He twisted to Megan. "I'm sorry Ma'am, did you see that touchdown? What an incredible game; I tell you: Big Boy Blue is a great running back. On the high-volume televisions, the WAGA sports reporter pointed the microphone to Blue. "Big Boy Blue, what an awesome game. We remember when you played for Eden High School in Atlanta; we hoped you would have attended Georgia Tech. Do you think the Atlanta Falcons can convince you to come back home?" Sweat was dripping down his Herculean twenty-year-old face. "My manager is my momma; she won't let me in the South unless the price is right. Besides, there is only one thing I want in Atlanta, Baby, and it ain't football." Blue blazed off. "Well folks, the 61st Rose Bowl game is over, but Super Bowl IX is in eleven days, I'll see you there."

A stunned Megan was silent. "Ma'am, about this RCA, the best feature is…"

"There is nothing I want to buy."

"But Ma'am, would you take my card, for the next time?" Her credit card was closed in her hand bag; she hurried to the parking garage.

"It can't be five o'clock." She glanced at her Lady Hamilton's wedding anniversary watch, "Why did I leave home?" She cried while speeding out.

"There is was no way I can beat this rush hour traffic." She remained quiet at the red light. The radio was playing the Four Tops, "Aint No Woman Like the One I've Got." She turned it off. Fifteen minutes passed, traffic started to move, and she headed south. And then, more traffic, she waited. Her mind was dead calm. She took a deep breath, stared at her fresh face in the mirror, and rolled down her window. Suddenly, the spring weather changed into a winter chill. The breeze refreshed her skin and spirit; traffic eased up.

Turning on Chester Street at five-thirty, Megan unclasped her antique pearl hair clip. "I love this hair clip; I remember when John gave it to me on my thirty-eighth birthday. Three months later I met Blue."

She drove steady in her drive way. "Baby, you don't need a new television set; you never have time to watch the one we got." She paused, "I got, yes I got, the man I want."

Mondays were Megan's vacuuming day. The Monday after John's birthday, she was vacuuming John Jr.'s white shag rug. The telephone rang. "Hello," she said.

"In each moment, they were our moments, I loved being with you. I am not going to let you go, I can't." Big Boy Blue became quiet. Megan was serene in her moment; she hung with the phone.

The following spring, Big Boy Blue was in his junior year at The Ohio State University. He was lying on his back, longing for her. "I know, I said I would not call you, Megan, but I can't sleep. I can have a different girl in the sunlight, moonlight, any night. What good is that if I can't have the woman I love?"

It was ten o'clock in the morning. "I need a game plan to win Megan back." He walked down his dorm hallway, picked up the pay phone, made a collect call to the only person who was more cold-bloodied than he. "Mom, it's your son; can we talk?"

The next day, Blue departed the Buckeye dorm on his way to Atlanta. His agent arranged for Dave El car service to meet him at Hartsfield Airport. "Take me to Chester Street." He eased in the exclusive, black sedan with black-tinted windows, becoming accustomed to his black American Express card. He tried to relax by listening to the music on the pop station, but he fidgeted in the back seat. "Will she talk to me? Will she let me explain? I can't take not having her. I need to know if she still loves me. If she is there, I'll see her eyes and know."

The speed was slow; he studied the street he lived on two and a half years ago. "Park the car across from the yellow house; I want to sit here and wait."

"Yes, sir," do you mind if the radio is on, sir."

"No, just be quiet. I'll let you know if I don't like something." He said bluntly; sighed impatiently. "Megan's house, but where is she?" He saw two glistened '68 Mustangs, one red, one white in the driveway. There was a new white wooden fence that separated her house from his Aunt Rose; yellow tulips were planted in the front yard. He stretched his head; saw a garden, tools, water sprinkling the yard. He heard her voice. "John, I'm in the back. Bring the soil bag; it's too heavy for me to carry."

"And there she is, my Baby," he murmured to himself. "The sun is shining on her naturally beautiful face, her round loving eyes sweetens the sun." He inspected her blue-denim halter top, Levi ankle-length jeans. "She looks younger, better than the same." Her pretty smile pleased him, pained him. His mouth pranced closer to the tinted glass. "She's my baby," he yowled inside his brain.

She grabbed her garden tools. John came out holding a wheel barrow. In it was a large soil bag. He opened it and spread it throughout the garden. They were laughing, working together. Blue laid his head toward the ceiling. "Why does she want him, when she can have me?"

"Sir, is this your last stop?" The driver asked.

"I'm paying you $50.00 an hour; what do you care? Don't worry about it."

He saw his Aunt Rose come to the back screen door; she waved her hand to John. "John, could you help me with this door? It keeps locking when I want it to open."

"Sure, Mrs. Rose, I'm on my way." Megan didn't notice. She grabbed her tools and walked closer to the front.

"I could run over, if her husband goes into the house," Blue thought. "That's all I need is a moment to be with her."

John, in tall rubber boots, ran across to Mrs. Rose.

"Darn, it," Megan said.

"What happened?" John asked. "Mrs. Rose, I'll be right back."

He rushed to her, look at her cut finger, kissed it, she kissed him.

He took out a white handkerchief from his pocket, wrapped her finger, and tied it into a bow. She laughed; he landed a kiss on her forehead.

"John son," Mrs. Rose, said. "I'll be right back.

"Okay, Mrs. Rose." John's hands were clinched all over Megan's waist; he led her finger in the house.

Blue's body barked at the world, he closed his eyes, and listened to the music. His mind was mute.

"Driver, take me back."

"Back, sir, where?" politely, he said.

"Where the fuck did you pick me up from? I want to get the hell out of Atlanta."

The driver flew to I-20; the music moved in Blue's subconscious mind. "Roll the windows down," Blue said to the driver, starring at the dark-blue sky.

"Yes, sir," he said, and turned straight to Delta Airlines departing flights.

A folded first class ticket in his pocket, he slammed the door. "Got to Be There," Michael Jackson's voice was ringing in his ears, "Oh, Baby, Got to Be There." "Megan," Blue said. "I got to be there, Baby, I got to be with you."

24

The Pittsburgh Steelers defeated the Dallas Cowboys twenty-one to seventeen at the Orange Bowl in Miami, Florida on January 18, 1976. It was Super Bowl X, and even though it was an easy game for the Steelers, it was torture for Big Boy Blue, the Steelers' running back.

Never for a moment did Blue Bedford doubt he would get his Super Bowl ring—even if it was the worst game of his life. He waited until just about everyone left the team's locker room; and tired to forget the sour pain in his knee.

Dr. Hartman applied bandages on his right knee.

"Blue, your leg is bad, but you will be fine in eight weeks, plenty of time to rest, heal before the coach needs you at practice in March. How old are you now?"

"Twenty-one," Blue said. "Why you want to know?"

"Because, you just had your first Super Bowl victory; and you are not celebrating with your teammates."

"What do I need them for?" He thought, "I need my baby; it's been three years since I've loved Megan." He reached for the telephone. In a second, the security guard opened his door.

"Hey Blue."

"What?"

"A fine looking lady is here to see you, mighty fine."

"I'm hurt man, don't have time, send her away. What kind of music is that?" Blue asked.

"It's classical," Dr. Hartman paused. "I believe its Mozart's German Dance No.3."

"German like you, Doc. Hey, don't forget to change the station to rhythm and blues when you leave."

"I always do, Blue. Be still, and let me finish my work."

With a hard knock at the door, the security guard walked in. "Excuse me Blue, the lady insisted I tell you her name is Megan."

Broad hands pushed Dr. Hartman's white cotton jacket out of his way. He hopped from the bench. His contented face blazed at the security guard. In a snap of his left finger, he grimaced in reverse to the bench.

"You must stay off your leg, Blue, I have to change your bandage again. Do not move." Dr. Hartman agitated voice said.

"Hello Blue," her purr seized the room, passing the security guard.

"What do you want?"

"I want you Blue."

Doctor Hartman studied Savannah's beautiful brown glowing skin and sensed she was unlike the other women who longed for the muscled physique of Blue.

She moved closer to Blue. "Miss, you have to leave," the security guard said.

"Blue, do you want me to leave?" she asked.

"It's okay Marvin, she can stay." He stared into Savannah's green contact lenses. "Why did you say her name?"

"I was checking to see if she still has you."

"Well, what do you care?"

"I said I want you. I was seeing if she will ever stop being my competitor."

"How could she be your competitor, when you were never in the house?"

"Blue, you mean I never had your heart, but you were in my house."

"Are you in love, Savannah?"

"With you," she said.

"No Baby, with you?" he returned.

"Why... I should love you, I don't know," she said. "But I do."

"She is not as loud as before," Blue recalled. He glanced at her short little black dress, long black leather coat, maintained majorette's thighs.

"I was in Florida," she said, "and I thought I would visit my high school sweetheart."

"You were the prom queen; I was not your king."

He stared at her light blue eye shadow; burgundy lips, shoulder-length, blond natural weave. She stroked his hurt knee. "Savannah's hair is different," he thought. "Her eagerness is the same." He jiggled his leg; she jumped back.

"I'm sorry you are hurt. It was a great game. Can I help you?" Savannah asked assertively.

"Help?" he laughed. "Not, unless you are a doctor."

"I am in my first year at Florida State University College of Medicine. I drove from Tallahassee to see you."

Dr. Hartman stopped wrapping Blue's leg.

"Do you know Dr. E. Evans, the chief resident at the hospital?"

"Dr. Evans is my mentor; he is becoming as famous as Blue."

"Well, Blue, I'm finished with my work; I can leave you in good hands. Remember to stay off your leg. If the pain persists I can prescribe medicine, but why would I when you refuse to take an aspirin? I will see you in five days. Good evening, to you both. Your next championship title is 365 days away."

"He's used to championship games," Savannah said. "Certainly, he knows what to do. Isn't that right, Baby?" Blue gave Savannah one more look. Dr. Hartman changed the music, nodded, and closed the door. "Blue, let me give you what she can never give you."

"What is that, Savannah?"

She kissed his brittle lips. "If I were your wife, you would be loved, and no longer on the sidelines."

He rubbed his knee. "I am in a lot of pain, Savannah. Could you tell my driver outside that I may be a moment."

"Blue, I'm driving you to your hotel; we are going to need more than a moment, Baby." He watched her knee-high boots, her hands latched the door.

His broken-down back rested on the bench. Savannah took care of him. "She could never be for me what Megan is, but I might give her some time to try," he thought, closing his eyes.

She pleased him a second time; his memories were in Georgia. The Temptations' song played while his heart swam deep with the words:

Just my imagination once again runnin' way with me.

Tell you it was just my imagination runnin' away with me.

no, no, no, no, no, no, no, can't forget her

Just my imagination once again runnin' way with me.

Tell you it was just my imagination runnin' away with me.

Sharply, in a half-conscious state, "Megan," he repeated in his mind, "When I get rid of this one, I'm calling my baby."

25

From her dining room, Megan had been preparing for a house full of guests since four in the morning. Christmas December 1977 was the happiest of her life. The weather all month had been gorgeous, and this particular Sunday it was forecast to be a perfect Southern kind of day.

Family and friends were due to arrive at three-thirty that afternoon. John was exhausted from decorating the tree and went straight to bed at midnight. The house was quiet; Megan was writing her last-minute preparations on the carved-oak wood table from Charleston, South Carolina. John and she drove to Charleston in November, a second honeymoon surprise. She fell in love with the charm of antique shops across the Ashley River.

Megan looked up at the glass of the eighteenth-century, crystal chandelier, that Mother Ella and Father Duke had surprised them with for their Christmas present. Miss May Perry presented them with a twenty-six piece Wedgwood porcelain china set on Thanksgiving Day as an early gift. She smiled at their twenty-year old solid birch China Deck. "What generosity of my family," Megan said, "I'm so happy." The floral centerpiece of white tulips from Holland had arrived by special delivery two days ago. John mentioned to Handsome Joe, "They are Megan's favorite flower," and two weeks later, they arrived in time for Christmas. The entire house smelled like springtime. "I'm so happy," she said. She sipped her fresh-squeezed orange juice and tasted sliced Georgia's peaches in a glass bowl. "I love the smell of Christmas morning, the tranquility of planning my party. Let's see, where I should seat John's parents, Handsome Joe, Suzy Mae, their daughter, and two sons? Thanks goodness his mother Margaret is not coming or I would run out of space." She walked around the twenty-six-seat table to inspect the name cards. "I have to remind John to get the long-stem candles out of the truck of his car." The doorbell rang. "Who is that this early?" she thought. In haste, she strode, hesitated, and stopped.

"What am I worried about? It could not be Blue; his power is lost." She started to look through the glass, oval peek hole, instead heard a voice she adored.

"Mom, Dad, it's me; I don't have my key." John Jr. was standing in his full West Point Cadet regalia carrying three large duffle bags over his shoulders.

"John Jr., wait a minute." Megan ran to the wood handrails, her white polka-dot cherry shorts on her bedroom floor, she stepped right in. On the way down, she buttoned John's khaki Air Force shirt. Her red ribbon swooped along her silk hair and gave her sense of the Pony Express rushing to open the red door.

"John Jr., we were expecting you home at noon." He dropped his bags, hugged his mom. "Sweetheart, I can barely breathe."

"Mom, I wanted to surprise you and Dad. Where is Dad?"

"He's asleep; it's early."

"Yeah, but not for a military man," he grabbed his bags and tossed them near the twelve-foot evergreen Christmas tree. "Man, does this tree remind me of Central Park. Mom, these are the same ornaments from when I was four years old."

"Oh, don't get me started with your Dad's old fashioned Christmas tree. He stayed up all night decorating, changing his mind where it should go. He rearranged the furniture in the living room three times. Between your coming home and his best friend Handsome Joe, he's worked up. He finally went to sleep early this morning."

He strolled into the dining room and glanced at the splendor of the room. "It's good being home, and Christmas, at that."

"We are very proud parents to have our "Second Lieutenant Son" home for Christmas." Megan observed John Jr. of twenty-one years old as a man, an exact image of her husband. She pondered, "I don't see myself in him, but I know I'm somewhere." He had a handsome stature of a diplomat with his distinguished West Point dark-blue cutaway coat, scarlet facings, brass buttons, blue waist coat, tight pantaloons, and large cocked hat. "Why did I not see John in the same way, when he was the same man? The trials of an aged life, I suppose."

"Mom," he hugged her, kissed her on the cheeks. "I tell the guys how gorgeous my mom is, and when I show them my parent's picture, the first thing they say: Is she your younger sister?" He removed his hat and cast it on the canvas arm chair.

He walked in the manner of his father—his great grandfather's nose commanded his shiny black leather boots to the aroma of a familiar fragrance, her roasted turkey in the electric range oven. On the butcher block was a dream-world of desserts: golden yellow cake, Mississippi mud cake, cheese-cake, tea cakes, coconut, and pineapple. The walnut extension table paraded pecan pie, pecan tart, sweet potato pies, and her famous cherry pie.

"Mom, I'm hungry; what time is breakfast?"

"Breakfast is when your father wakes up. However, for my son, he can eat breakfast this minute." She opened the refrigerator and placed cheddar cheese and eggs on the round pedestal table.

"What about blueberry pancakes?"

"I keep blueberries in the house all year, just in case you fly in for breakfast."

He grabbed a bottle of chocolate milk. Megan smiled, reaching for a large glass bowl.

"Mom, you're not mad about Morehouse anymore are you? I know I asked you before, and you said you were okay. You know, as soon as I arrived at the Academy, I saw the comfort of home. There were officers who reminded me of my dad, his joy of being a fighter pilot, the honor he has serving his country." She was quiet while listening to him talk about his friends and professors.

She heated two cast-iron skillets; she mixed the pancake batter, emptied blueberries in a chestnut bowl. "Sweetheart, I left my orange juice in the dining room; could you bring it to me?" She paused, and then thought, "Does, John Jr. know about me and Blue? If he does, he never told his father, nor made me feel that he does."

He returned with a half-full glass of juice. "Hey Mom, our neighbor Blue may get his second ring. He gets traded to Dallas this year. And the Cowboys just might win the Super Bowl game next year. You probably wouldn't know since you hate football. Does he ever visit his aunt, Mrs. Rose?"

"What is he, psychic?" she thought. "No John Jr., Mrs. Rose doesn't remember her nephew; she has Alzheimer's like your Grandmother Lina had," she said, grabbing her juice from his hands.

"I'm sorry to hear that Mom." He scooped a handful of blueberries.

"She is in her late nineties and lives in an elderly home on Briarcliff Road. Your father and I visit her sometimes. More often, I go, sit, and bring her lunch. She seems to remember my cherry pies; she is so cute."

"That's good, Blue probably don't care anyway. I know he had a big crush on you; everybody on the block wanted you to be their mom."

Hastily, she said, "I think it was more of my pies and pan-fried chicken, especially, your paunchy friend Willie. Will he be stopping over for the holidays?"

"No, he's studying for exams at Georgia State University; he is determined to graduate from college next year."

She touched her stomach. "Ouch," she said.

"Mom, are you okay." He stared at her intensely.

"I'm fine, John Jr. Have a seat, and eat your breakfast. I'll wake your father."

"Wake me up? I'm up. How can I sleep with pancakes on the grill?"

"Dad," John Jr. said. They hugged. "Hey, you are pretty fit—too much work, huh?"

"Your mother has me working in the garden, hiking in national parks; the only time I rest is going to the base."

"How is the smartest guy I know, my son? What time did you get in? Hey, the uniform, not bad for a "butter ball," and he hugged John Jr. again.

"Thanks Dad, I try to represent you. I don't want to embarrass Colonel John Smith, sir." He saluted and hurried to his breakfast.

"Good morning." John kissed Megan. "Baby, I'll make the coffee; you got a big celebration later."

"How many people are coming for dinner?" John Jr. asked.

"Your mother invited everybody on Chester Street."

She laughed, slipped into her purple-plastic gloves, and proceeded to wash dishes. "John Jr., finish your breakfast, you too John, and leave the kitchen. I have to get everything ready. With John Jr. arriving early, Aunt May and her new boyfriend from Argentina, they will be here before I know it, not to mention my in-laws, John's friends from Louisiana; and I found out yesterday, your father invited Mr. Spriggs, and his bride Mary Bell. I have to cook and gift-wrap presents." She turned off the water, removed her gloves and faced husband and son.

John's firm hands came to Megan, kissed her left palm. "Baby you got your men here to help; give us a job—we are military men, we can handle anything." His warmhearted lips kissed her creamy lips.

"This is what I missed," John Jr. exclaimed, "seeing my loving parents."

"Son, speaking of love, when are you falling in love?"

"Dad, I've been eyeing someone, remember when you told me, some women have more luggage than others. Well, so far, they all got plenty. I'll let you guys know when the luggage is half-full." Everyone giggled.

She slipped away from John and turned the water back on. "Ouch," she hollered and touched her stomach. John Jr. jumped out of his seat and stepped near her.

"Baby, what's wrong?" John asked.

"Yeah, Mom," John Jr. said. Two pairs of frightened eyes were upon her. She smiled.

Father and son said. "No."

"Yes," she held John's hand. "Baby, I was planning to tell you last week. Dr. Némirovsky said, I should wait another week." John's hands rubbed her stomach.

"Baby, how many months?" he asked glowing and grinning.

"One month, gaining weight and it must be a girl, because she moves around a lot." She smiled at John; stared at John Jr. "Sweetheart, you're going to have a little brother or sister." Tears of merriment mesmerized the room.

Her husband kissed her gleeful cheeks.

"Wow, Mom, I'm going to be a big brother, what a Christmas!" He embraced his mom.

"Baby, we are going to have a baby." John's stable, strong handsome hands held her radiant face. Soft-hearted lips kissed his wife's nose, eyes, mouth.

"Mom, I think I'll rest before you give us our marching orders around the house." He held on to his plate. "I love you guys," John Jr. nodded his head and left them in the kitchen.

Neither heard a word. "I love you John," she said. He held her right, tight.

"I love you more," he said.

"Baby do you think I am too old to be a Dad? I'm 52." Her arms wrapped around his neck.

"What about me? I'm 42; how do you think I feel."

He drew her closer. "You make me feel young; you are my girl."

She removed his black cotton tee shirt. Her head rested on his solid chest, his hand loosened her red ribbon, and waves overflowed her back. He caressed her smooth legs high and unbuttoned her shorts.

"What about John Jr.?" she whispered.

"He knows his parents."

Her sultry lips were breathless in her man's chest. She paused, lifted her head. "I'm your girl."

"Yes, Baby, you're my girl."

Made in the USA
Columbia, SC
18 August 2022